TRANSUBSTANTIATION

MARY GRIMM

C&R Press
Conscious & Responsible

PRAISE FOR TRANSUBSTANTIATION

"Tender and spooky, humorous and wistful, *Transubstantiation* is a quiet, haunting study of characters who battle loneliness and thwarted dreams, but are often saved by their sheer will and imaginations. A heartbreakingly beautiful book."
-Thirty Umrigar, author of eleven novels, including *The Space Between Us*, *Honor*, and most recently, *The Museum of Failures*

"The epiphanic stories Mary Grimm constructs in the concentrated collection, *Transubstantiation*, are riddled with essential literary 'stares.' Grimm skillfully orchestrates, shifts, and shakes one subdued, understated, and sublime sacred stare after another. These profound glances glance then fix, siccing sight on the now exposed mechanisms of morality and mortality. These plied and implied visions vista the tectonic shifts in each fiction's universe, tweak the tweaks into a long, long ton of meaning and feeling. Yes, "stares" are general all over *Transubstantiation*, but they are essential for readers to inhabit the moment when, instantly, the familiar becomes this *this*, the familiar defamiliarized italicized instant."
-Michael Martone, author of *Plain Air: Sketches from Winesburg, Indiana* and *The Complete Writings of Art Smith, The Bird Boy of Fort Wayne*, Edited by Michael Martone

"The stories in Mary Grimm's *Transubstantiation* introduce us to the seemingly plain lives of female characters with such tenderness and care that they become remarkable. Pinpointing the strange and unknowable nestled inside the familiar is what Mary Grimm does better than any other writer I have read. In these urgent, humane stories of treacherous childhoods, adult loneliness, the entwined yet disperate lives of sisters, ill-fated couplings and burgeoning hope, we find Grimm's compassionate humor and sensuality, and the promise for longed-for truth. With an ingenious gift with nuance and detail, and a master playwright's gift with funny-sad dialogue, Grimm offers each of her characters the kind of flawed, beautiful agency we can identify with."
-Meg Pokrass, author of eight flash fiction collections, two collections of hybrid prose, and two novellas-in-flash, including her most recent, *The Loss Detector* and *Spinning to Mars*

TRANSUBSTANTIATION

Contents

DOVE AND ELLIE

Ellie's mother, Dove, believed in family, even though hers had let her down. She never saw her sister, who had moved to a different state without telling anyone, and her brother was dead. "I don't know them anymore, and they don't know me," she said to Ellie.

Ellie was sometimes resentful about this lack of relationships. No grandmother with white permed hair, no grandfather with a fishing hat. No aunts and uncles, no family reunion picnics with baked beans and Jello salad. All they had for a family was Rudy who was her mother's cousin once removed, although no one could explain to Ellie what he was removed from.

Ellie sat with her mother in the front room, her face to the yellow sun that poured out of the summer air. Her mother was in the rocking chair, leaning forward to hold Ellie by the shoulders.

"There are bad people in the world," she said to Ellie.

"Who?" Ellie asked.

"Nobody in particular." Her mother paused to consider. "Most people are good. But there are some bad ones, too."

"So?" Ellie was bored. The sun was coming in hard through the window, lighting up the lampshade as if the lamp were turned on. The bars of light burst through the back of the rocking chair, striping the side of her mother's face.

"Listen to me, will you? You're eight years old. You're going to a new school in the fall." Ellie's mother raised her hands and let them fall back into her lap. "There are people around who'd hurt you if they could."

Ellie believed that her mother was talking about Ellie's father, who had hurt Dove many years ago, when Ellie was born or shortly after. All that Ellie knew about him was that he could whistle "The Star Spangled Banner," and that his eyes were silver.

This was something that her mother argued about with her cousin Rudy, Rudy insisting that they were only gray, a plain gray.

"If he comes around, I won't talk to him," Ellie assured her mother.

"If who comes around?"

"Whoever," Ellie said. She was tired of kneeling and she twisted in her mother's hands. "Can I go outside?"

Dove was making a pie for dinner, which she did whenever Rudy came over. Rudy sat and watched her thumbs and forefingers crimp the pie crust together round the edge, a pinching motion that she made over and over, each pinch a perfect scallop. "Remember when grandma made pie?" she said.

Rudy followed her fingers with his eyes, feeling a little dreamy, pleasantly disconnected. "No," he said.

"Don't you remember coming here to play? Her garden with the wooden tomato cages? the cat that slept in the bathroom?" Dove lived in her grandmother's house, left to her, the favorite grandchild.

"I don't remember nothing of a cat."

"Her name was Mitzi," Dove said, her fingers pinching, pinching.

Rudy shook his head. "Where's Ellie?"

"She's next door, watching TV with Mrs. Knapik."

Rudy shook his head again, this time in disbelief. "What for?"

"They like to watch the soaps together."

Rudy smacked the table as if he were going to say something angry, and Dove looked at him nervously. Instead, he got up and poured himself a glass of milk from the fridge. "I'm starting a new job tomorrow. Night shift. Electronics."

Dove nodded, spooning pie filling into the crust. "Ellie will miss you," she said. The filling, custardy and sweet, filled the pie perfectly, lapping at the scalloped edge.

"Can't be helped." Rudy put the glass down on the drainboard with a clink.

Next door, Ellie and Mrs. Knapik sat on her sofa bed with the afghan over their knees. On the tv screen a woman was standing in front of a big painting that looked just like her except in old-fashioned clothes. "Who are you?" the woman said to the picture.

"It's her, isn't it?" Ellie asked.

"Sshh," Mrs. Knapik said.

"It's like her evil twin, right? Her evil, old-fashioned twin."

"Maybe so," Mrs. Knapik said.

The woman on the screen turned as someone came into the room. "What are you doing here?" she said.

Mrs. Knapik put her hands over Ellie's ears so that she could hear only blurs of sound, bleats coming from first one, then the other's lips. "She's having his baby, right?" Ellie said. "But he doesn't know it."

"Smarty-pants." The commercial came on and Mrs. Knapik took her hands away. "Hand me a miniature Snickers, will you, sweetie?"

Mrs. Knapik spent all day on the sofa bed and then at night she went upstairs to her regular bed. She wasn't supposed to eat candy because she had sugar in her blood, but she and Ellie had a pact about this, as well as about Ellie's secret dog which she fed and played with in Mrs. Knapik's garage.

"You would think she'd be smarter than to go for him all over again, wouldn't you?" Mrs. Knapik said to Ellie as the woman appeared again on the screen. She was looking in a meaningful way at a different man, with thicker eyebrows and ears that stuck out a little.

Ellie considered this. Was this man one of the bad people? Should she be looking out for someone like him? She knew they were all actors, really, although sometimes when she was talking to Mrs. Knapik, she forgot. His eyebrows were a little scary, she thought. She watched as the woman stepped forward and they kissed in a sloppy way. Ellie knew, in spite of Mrs. Knapik's censoring hands, that this meant that they were going to have sex. If not right now, then soon. If she was lucky, she'd get a peek at it.

Rudy sat in the driveway for a minute, looking in the window at Dove washing the dishes. Her head was tipped back a little, her sandy hair falling away from her face, and her lips were moving. She was singing along with the radio. Half the pie lay beside him on the seat, wrapped in plastic. He could see the light in Ellie's room upstairs, and her shadow against the curtains, jumping like a monkey. Mrs. Knapik's house was lit up, too. She liked to have the lights on at night, he knew from Ellie, even after she'd gone up to sleep. Rudy drummed his fingers on the wheel as he watched the bluish light of Mrs. Knapik's tv flare and die back again as the picture changed from one thing to another. He had once been a burglar. He had been in jail for this, years ago, before Ellie was born. It wasn't something he planned on doing again, but sometimes the desire came back. Not for the cash so much or the small electronics, so easy to sell, but for the step over the threshold, or through the window, the step that took him from one world to another. His fingers itched to slide into a drawer, feeling among the silks and cottons for what was hidden there, a coin collection, an expensive pair of earrings, a watch. Even when the things he found were useless, he loved the finding of them, the deck of cards decorated with naked women, the dried-up rose pressed in a sleeve of waxed paper. Once he had found a nest of small rocks in a woman's sock drawer--five black rocks, cool, oval, and smooth. He still carried one of them in his pocket, all this time later. Watching Mrs. Knapik's tv light shift like the aurora, he wondered what was in her drawers, so long a widow, so generous with store cookies and quarters for Ellie. He breathed out quickly, a loud harrumph, and started up the car.

Downstairs, Dove washed the dishes slowly, thinking of her mother and her grandmother, both dead. Her mother's hair had been silvery blonde, a few shades lighter than Dove's. The most beautiful woman in the world, her father had said to her when she was eighteen, her mother dead for more than ten years. She was grateful for this memory, for how his face had changed when he said it, his mouth working a little, his eyes narrowing as if to shut out some great light, the light of her mother's past loveliness. You'll never be the beauty your mother was, he'd said to Dove, who had only resented this a little at the time. Her hands moved gracefully in the dish water, washing each dish, rinsing it, setting it carefully to dry as if it were china, painted with flowers and rimmed with gold. The dishes, mismatched, cracked and stained, gleamed with water until they dried.

Late in the night, Mrs. Knapik arose from her upstairs bed and walked across the bedroom floor, her nightgown sweeping behind her, her hair long and white around her face. Her eyes were half open as if she hardly needed to see, as if the dark were full of light. At the door to the hall, she paused, touching the doorjamb, running her hand down the wood as if looking for cracks, and then she went out into the hall and down the stairs, searching for each step with her bare foot, her hand sliding down the banister. In the front room, where she had left the light on earlier, she stood as if she were looking out the window, but there was only the white expanse of the blind. Still, she stood there and looked at it, her eyes wide and blank. Sometimes she stood until morning, until the thump of the paper against her door, but this time she stayed downstairs only for a little more than an hour before she went back to bed.

"The dresses were gold," Dove told Ellie. "There were three bridesmaids, one blonde, one dark-haired, one with reddish hair."

Ellie nodded, satisfied by this variety. "What was the groom wearing?"

"They always wear the same thing." Dove had been to play the organ for a wedding, one of her jobs, and now she was hemming Ellie's uniform skirt before she went to run the cash register at the corner store, another job. Ellie stood on a chair while Dove pinned her up with silver pins.

"That's what I'll be doing," Ellie said. "Wearing the same thing as everyone else. But it's OK," she said when Dove looked worried. "Did they all cry?"

"The mothers cried, and one of the bridesmaids cried."

"Not the other two?"

"No," Dove said, tweaking at the skirt to make the pleats lie flat.

"Maybe they're the wicked bridesmaids. Like wicked stepsisters. Maybe one of them is having a baby with the groom."

"Don't be silly," Dove said.

"No one would know," Ellie assured her. "Not unless they get the DNA."

Dove felt that Ellie was getting away from her. She felt that if Rudy were around more this wouldn't be happening. "Rudy's going on the night shift," she said to Ellie.

"I know," Ellie said. She stood while her mother took the skirt off her and then she started to dance on the chair, swiveling her hips in their pale blue underpants.

"Stop that, will you," Dove said.

"I've got to boogie," Ellie said. "Don't you know."

Outside, summer had gotten sticky and wet. Ellie lay under the bridal wreath bush and waited for the sweat to drip off her nose. She had positioned herself above an ant, waiting to strike it with the monsoon Ellie. Too soon, the ant stopped fussing around with a breadcrumb and scurried off. Ellie flopped over. From here, she could see the back of her house, like a cliff or a wave about to roll over on her. She closed her eyes and then opened them quickly, as if surprised by the house-wave. It gave her a dizzy feeling in her stomach, like a ride at the fair, and she did it several more times, until it wore off. It was almost time to go to Mrs. Knapik's, but she didn't move. She could see into the back yard of the people behind them. They had a swing set and two girls and a boy--all new since last year. A week ago she had spied on them through the fence while they played on the swings and in the attached sand box. The biggest of them was short compared to Ellie, only up to her shoulder. They were babies. She wasn't sorry she was going to a new school. The kids at her old school were all babies. On her hands and knees, she crawled out from under the bush, and then across the yard, feeling the soft grass under her hands, and then the gravel of the driveway, and then Mrs. Knapik's grass and her slate sidewalk. She crawled up the steps and knocked on the screen door without getting up. When Mrs. Knapik came and said "Who is it?" she jumped up. Mrs. Knapik shrieked and put her hand on her heart, but then she laughed. "You'll give me an attack. And then who would you watch tv with?"

Ellie couldn't imagine.

Inside, they settled on the sofa, Mrs. Knapik with her afghan over her knees. She was often chilly, even in the summer because, she had told Ellie, her blood was thin. Ellie picked up Mrs. Knapik's hand to look at her rings. "The engagement ring, the wedding ring, the first anniversary ring," she said, naming them. "The ring when you went to New Orleans, the ring when you had the big fight." Five in all, four more than Dove had. On TV a woman was sitting on a couch, her legs crossed, drinking something dark from a glass. "Todd must never know," she said, and pursed her lips together.

"Dove told me about the bad people," Ellie said to Mrs. Knapik, who shook her head sadly. Ellie waited to see if Mrs. Knapik would say something, but she kept her eyes on the tv, where the woman was looking through pictures in an album while another woman spied on her from the hall. Ellie couldn't understand why she didn't just turn around and catch her watching. "Do you know any bad people?" she asked.

Mrs. Knapik shook her head some more, wagging it like the dog Rudy had once had in the back window of his car. "I don't like that kind of talk," she said to Ellie. "I don't know what your mother is thinking." She paused, considering. "She knows best though, remember that. Your mother knows best."

"It's because of going to a new school. I'm going to have to walk farther. I'll have to wear a uniform and we'll have religion class."

"Blessed Sacrament," Mrs. Knapik said, nodding now. The woman had put aside the album and was now talking on the phone. "Todd," she said, "I have to see you."

"Most people are good," Mrs. Knapik said, turning down the sound as the commercial came on. She sat, her fingers tapping the buttons on the remote. "Did I ever tell you about when I had my purse stolen on the bus?"

"Mmhmm," Ellie said. "He slid it out from under your hand."

"As smooth as butter. Oh, my." Mrs. Knapik put her hand out, feeling for the bowl with the miniature Snickers bars.

"I don't have a purse," Ellie observed. "But I might get one when I go to the new school, don't you think?"

"You might. A red one, maybe?"

"Red," Ellie said, agreeing. She laid her head against Mrs. Knapik's shoulder, even though it was too hot and watched as the woman, back now after the commercial, opened the door for Todd. Before she could say anything, he put his arms around her and kissed her. Ellie sat up, in case this led to anything exciting.

Just then, Dove was letting herself into the back door of their house. Her arms were trembling from the weight of the grocery bags she was carrying. She'd been going to take the bus, but a woman she didn't know had offered her a ride, and she had accepted, because she had bought so many things in cans. In the car, Dove had told the woman how her mother had died just that morning. "I haven't even told my little girl," she said, and the woman made sympathetic noises. "Or her brother either." Dove had imagined this boy as younger than Ellie, no more than a baby really. "It was her heart," she said to the woman. She couldn't seem to stop herself. "A hemorrhage, the doctor said."

"Isn't there a test for that?" the woman had asked.

"She didn't have any symptoms," Dove said.

"You poor, poor thing."

"My husband always hated her," Dove said. "He said he won't even go to the funeral, just the wake."

The woman shook her head in sympathy.

Now, Dove took the cans out of the bags and lined them up on the table, thinking spaghetti tonight, beef stew tomorrow, leftovers on Thursday. Ellie wouldn't eat the beef in the stew, but she would get the good of the juices. Dove could pick some lettuce for a salad, some cucumbers, a tomato. Rudy had started on the night shift, but he might stop by late. Dove put on the radio and danced around the kitchen, putting things away, swinging her hips and singing in her golden voice. When she sang in the choir, her voice sounded holy, she knew. Like an angel, people in the church had said to her. But singing along with the radio, she hoped it sounded more earthly. Sexy. She opened her mouth wide so that the sound belled out, reaching up to the high shelves. In the garden, she hummed through her closed lips, thinking of the wedding she had been to last week, the lowered lids of the bridesmaids, the rich folding of the bride's gown as she knelt at the altar. Dove imagined herself kneeling that way, the whitened soles of her shoes showing under the froth of her skirt. She would have the longest train anyone could imagine, the longest veil, the whitest lace, the most sparkling ring. She picked enough tomatoes for Mrs. Knapik, who never cooked for herself any more, putting the warm tomatoes into the front of her blouse and pulling the hem up to hold them. She turned toward her neighbor's house and saw Ellie coming out the side door, dragging her feet across the grass.

"I have to go out tonight," Dove said. "Just for a little while. I'm going to sing a set with Rudy's friend's band."

Ellie nodded her head, trying to imitate how Mrs. Knapik did it, with a little tremble at the end of each nod.

Mrs. Knapik leaned over the end of the sofa, looking out the window at Ellie and her mother. My, they looked sweet together, she thought. Sweet. The tv talked in a mumble behind her, but all her attention was on Ellie dancing from foot to foot, Dove smoothing down her hair with one hand, holding the front of her blouse up with the other. She could see their mouths move, as if they were in a silent movie.

"Love," she thought she saw Dove say, which was nice, love between a mother and daughter, or between anyone, for that matter. Mrs. Knapik sank back into the cushions of the sofa and sighed.

"Don't listen to her," she told the man on the tv screen, who was listening to the woman in the evening gown with a bemused expression. "She's a two-face," she advised him. Mrs. Knapik had never owned an evening gown, but she had had some very nice dresses, very nice indeed. The powder-blue rayon she'd worn for her forty-fifth anniversary, for instance. Why not wait and have a party on your fiftieth, her sister had said. "If I'd listened to her, I'd have missed out." She paused, watching the man on the tv watch the woman who was putting on lipstick very slowly. "He died on me, didn't he." She shook her head, thinking of the powder-blue rayon dress, with its little raised collar, its satin buttons, the tricky draping of the bodice that gave her a certain fullness at the bosom. Your bosom was supposed to fill out when you had children, but they hadn't been blessed.

"Mrs. K!" Ellie burst into the house. "I brought you tomatoes."

"Set them on the table, dear," Mrs. Knapik said. "I'll make them into a nice salad." She listened to Ellie run down the hall, the thump of the tomatoes onto the table, the slap of Ellie's bare feet on the linoleum. "Get that pack of Oreos, will you honey? and put them into a bowl for us."

"Mom's going to sing tonight," Ellie told her when she was settled on the sofa beside her.

"Oh, how we danced on the night we were wed," Mrs. Knapik sang. "It's a song," she told Ellie.

"She'll probably sing newer songs," Ellie said.

"I suppose so." Mrs. Knapik took an Oreo from the bowl and twisted the two halves apart so she could lick the creamy center.

At the bar, Rudy sat on a stool under the tv and watched Dove prepare to sing a song with the band. It was a band that played country and whatever else appealed to the lead singer, a fat man who wore cowboy boots and a derby hat. His weight was causing back problems, he was telling Dove on stage while the others tuned their guitars. "An operation would kill me," he said, and Dove nodded, smiling, her fingers braiding the strips of leather fringe on her jacket. "They give me this here." Rudy saw him pull out something that looked like a tv remote. "It gives me an electric shock, you know? If it gets too bad, I just zap myself." He laughed, and Rudy watched, fascinated, as his belly rolled and shivered inside his pearl-snapped shirt.

The bartender held up his arm and pointed at his watch. The singer hoisted himself off his stool and picked up the microphone, which squawked briefly. "Hey, everyone," he said, smiling. "Listen, we're back. And here's a little lady who's going to take over for this old cowboy for a spell. Her name's Dove, and she's as sweet as a dove, isn't she? Give her a big hand, why don't y'all?" He got himself back up on the stool and pulled a harmonica out of his pocket, nodding to Dove.

Dove stepped forward, smiling, her hands clasped in front of her. Rudy thought she looked like an orphan, her jacket too big, her light hair frizzed out around her face. She was wearing a pair of high heels that made her lean slightly forward. "Hi," she said.

"Hi beautiful," someone said from the back, and Rudy turned around to see who it was.

"Hi," Dove said again. The bar noise surged up and over her, and Rudy wanted to look away. "I'm going to sing 'Old Flames,'" she said, and then added, "'Old Flames Don't Hold a Candle to You.' It's an old song but I hope you'll like it." She pulled the microphone out of its holder and held it clasped at her chin.

When she started singing Rudy was surprised at how big her voice came out. He usually heard her singing in the kitchen, or occasionally when she made him go to church, and he thought of her voice as pleasant, a thread of sound that was personal and intimate. But here in the bar her voice had more sound in it, as if she was standing at the mouth of a cave, the air behind her buoying her up and pushing the words out before her. She clasped her hands around the mike as if she were in church, praying, and her knees were pressed together. He could see the whiteness on her knuckles. Her voice had taken on a quaver that was never there in church, for sure, and which made the men at the bar turn around and take another look at her, looking for the place in her that started that quivering. "No shit," Rudy said to himself.

"Now that was real nice," the lead singer was saying, "Let's give her a hand, can we?" He clapped his hands heavily, his remote zapper hanging from his wrist.

"Do you remember how I sang for the talent show in fifth grade?" Dove said in the car on the way home. "My mother made me a dress for it." When Rudy didn't answer she asked again. "Do you remember that?" It had been pink, the ruffles hand-sewn, starched and pressed with the iron until they bloomed like a rose.

"You won." Rudy turned the car sharply at the corner to their street.

"I did, didn't I?" Dove smiled. "But do you remember that dress?" She turned in the seat to look at him. "Do you remember my mother, Rudy?"

Rudy pulled into the driveway. "Why wouldn't I?" he said. His hands were still on the wheel and Dove knew he was waiting for her to say, come in, why don't you? Come in and have a cup of coffee. Come and lie on my pillow.

Ellie sat in the middle of the Mrs. Knapik's upstairs hall, listening. She had read a book about two children who found a ghost, and she wanted to try it. The most likely places, she felt, would be the basement or the attic. But the steps to Mrs. Knapik's attic pulled down, which she wasn't tall enough to do, and she was afraid of the basement. Mrs. Knapik was half sleeping in front of the tv, the colors on the screen washing over her. The upstairs hall was a little spooky with the lights off, but not too bad. The light from the streetlight came in through the front bedroom. Ellie climbed up on the bed carefully and lay back on one of the pillows. "Oh, darling," she said. She turned her head toward the other pillow. "You are amazing." She rolled around on the bed for a minute and then got up, smoothing over where she'd been. She sat down on the hall floor, crossing her legs.

She wouldn't mind some children to hunt ghosts with, someone her own age or older. Ellie had made up stories to herself about a family moving in next door. a family with a boy and a girl. The girl would be just Ellie's age, eight, the boy a year younger, so they could boss him around. Ellie had written in her notebook a list of the games they would play and where their hideout would be. She would even let them in on the secret dog, probably.

Ellie closed her eyes and waited. She could hear the drip of the bathroom tap, and a car going by outside. In the book, the children had been alerted to the presence of the ghosts by music, and she strained to hear anything like that. The carpet in the hall scratched her legs. What would I do if a robber came in here? she thought, someone like the one who tried to steal Mrs. K's purse. You could use your credit card to open doors, she knew. You cut wires to mess up the alarm system. But Mrs. K didn't have one. The robber would look for valuables. "He didn't get my valuables," Mrs. K had said. Money or jewelry.

Her eyes closed, Ellie thought of her father, that bad person. He wasn't dead, she was pretty sure, because her mother would have told her. Dove was a truthful person. He would be living far away, in a cabin in a forest maybe, chopping wood for a fire. She imagined him chopping down a tree so big that the top could not be seen. The beginnings of its fall were invisible, the leaves and branches cutting through the air with a sound like violins, high-pitched and squealing.

Downstairs, the hot summer air of the day was cooling, currents silently dividing around her bare ankles. Mrs. Knapik's hands were clasped before her like Dove's on the microphone. She looked as if she were thinking about something important, something she might do in the next moment, her lips pursed with concentration. Her hair, which she always braided before she went to bed, had come half undone. It fanned across her back, white and feathery over the padded, curved bones of her shoulders and spine. Her knees trembled a little with the strain of standing so still. On the tv, a pair of otters were tumbling and spinning in the froth of a waterfall.

The next day Ellie's eyes felt heavy. She had awaked in her own bed, but still wearing her clothes. Her mother sang at breakfast, and she sang when she pushed Ellie out the door to play. "Go and talk to those kids back there. Maybe they'll want to play with you," she had said.

Ellie examined them through the screen of the lilac bush at the back of the yard. Babies, she thought. One of them was crying in their sandbox, and another was banging a shovel against the trunk of a little tree. The third one was nowhere to be seen. Ellie made a little noise, experimentally, a string of ooohs that rose musically. Putting her hands around her mouth, she did it again, trying to make it sound like something a ghost would say. "Oooooh," she moaned, keeping well back in the bush. The baby in the sandbox turned to look toward Ellie, tears still rolling down her cheeks. "Ooohooh. Ooooheeyooh." Ellie made a scrabbling noise in the bush, rattling one branch against another. The shovel-banger stopped and turned his head. Ellie thrust her hands out of the bush and waved them like pompoms without showing her face. "Mom!" he screamed. He threw his shovel down and ran into the house, leaving the baby behind. "Oooh," Ellie called to her more softly, singing without words. She looked back at the bush, but didn't move. Still looking, she began to suck her thumb.

Babies, Ellie thought. She backed out of the bush and sidled along the yard to Mrs. Knapik's garage, opening the green-painted door and sliding inside as if she were a spy. She sat on the floor and waited. The garage was empty, had been empty as long as Ellie could remember. Once Mrs. Knapik had had a car, her husband's car, but she couldn't drive, and so finally she sold it. Ellie could smell the car although it was gone. Its smell, like the gas station, like something burning, was still here, a ghost of a smell. The floor was hardpacked dirt, and she put her hands down to feel its coolness. The air was dim, green with the leaves pressed against the windows. She could hear her mother calling but she didn't move, waiting, her eyes half closed. Soon she could hear a scratching, a tapping against the dirt. She put her hands out, curved to fit around a dog's head. They liked to be scratched behind the ears, she knew. The dog's name was Star.

"Ellie! Ellie!" Dove called, her voice rising.

Ellie squinted. Carefully, she moved her hand through the air, remembering the feel of the police dog she'd petted at school, a long time ago, last year. The dog had felt warm, his skin sliding over his bones, the glossy hair smooth against her palm. Fiercely, she remembered that now.

"Rudy's going to stay here tonight," Dove said. She was comb-ing her hair and looking at herself in the mirror. "I have to work for Cindy."

Ellie sat on the bed behind her. "Is Cindy sick?"

"Probably." Dove tucked in her shirt, which had her name on the pocket, and "Convenient Food Mart" in red letters. Dissatisfied, she pulled it out again. The card the man in the bar had given her was on the tray where she kept her nail polish. "What would you think if we moved some day?"

"I don't want to move." Ellie had picked up her mother's per-fume and was pretending to spray herself with it.

"But what if we did? If I didn't have to work at the store any more. People don't live their whole lives in the same place." Dove thought of her family, scattered like a handful of seed. "You'd have new friends, maybe."

"I'm already going to a new school," Ellie said, as if this were all that could be asked of her.

Dove came and sat next to her on the bed. "Oh, Ellie."

"Would he come and live with us?" Ellie said, thinking of her father. She imagined him packing his suitcase, closing the door to the log cabin, walking through the woods.

Dove looked at her, startled. "Who?" She smoothed her hand over the pillow, her heart beating faster. "You mean Rudy?"

"I don't know," Ellie said. She slid down the side of the bed and ran downstairs. Dove looked after her without moving. The air was heavy, waiting to rain. She put on her shoes and stood up to look in the mirror again, fluffing her hair out with her hands and smoothing it over her shoulders. She saw the bed behind her, the spread rucked up, and she blushed.

Rudy made macaroni and cheese from a box, which Ellie loved, and they sat at the kitchen table eating it. Rudy had brought in the little tv and they watched Wheel of Fortune while they ate. "Mrs. K is good at guessing the phrases," she told him. "She'd win for sure if she went on. But she says she doesn't need the aggravation or the money."

Rudy pushed the dish of sliced tomatoes Dove had left for them in the refrigerator across the table. "Got to eat your vegetables."

"Tomatoes are fruits," Ellie told him. "I saw it on tv." She sat chewing, looking at Rudy. He was smoking a cigarette, his chair balanced on its back legs. "We could make a pie out of them if they're fruits, right?"

Rudy was looking out the window, but there was nothing there to see.

"Mrs. K says she'll eat anything in a pie." Ellie slurped in a spoonful of noodles.

Rudy snorted. "I'll bet she would."

"Are you going to come and live with us in a new house?" Ellie kept her eyes on her plate, but she could see Rudy out of the corners.

Rudy thumped his chair down on the floor. "What are you talking about? What new house?"

"I don't know," Ellie said. She stabbed a tomato with her fork and watched the juice blend in with the cheese sauce—a milky pink color. "Do you know any bad people?"

"What the hell are you talking about?" They stared at each other for a minute, Ellie's fork resting in her hand, Rudy's palms flat on the table.

"You're a crazy kid, you know? You watch too much tv."

"I like tv," Ellie said. Her forehead felt tight.

"You shouldn't spend so much time over there with the old woman."

"She's my best friend," Ellie said. She put the fork down and pushed her plate away.

Rudy studied her for a minute, looking as if he were going to say something else, and Ellie waited, holding her breath. "Shit," he said. "Come on, let's go for a ride. We'll get some ice cream."

Ellie got up and took his hand when he held it out. "Chocolate," she said, "with a dip."

After Ellie was asleep, Rudy went outside and stood in the driveway, smoking another cigarette. The streetlight was shaded by the leaves of the sycamore tree and it was almost dark between the houses. Mrs. Knapik's tv had been turned off a while ago, and her house was silent, although the lights were still on. Running up the electricity, crazy old woman. He stubbed his cigarette out and held himself still, listening, rubbing the tips of his fingers together. A car went by and then another. Rudy waited several moments longer and then walked up the porch steps. As if he were thinking, he paused, then grasped the screen door knob, using his handkerchief. When it opened, he nodded, and paused again, holding his body still. Slowly he put his fingers on the doorknob and turned it, a fraction at a time. To his surprise, it was open. He pushed it, the handkerchief between his palm and the wood, and slipped inside.

The tv was off, the couch in front of it abandoned, an afghan thrown over the back. A mixing bowl of candy sat askew among the cushions. No wonder Ellie had cavities, he thought. He looked around without moving, his back against the door. Everything looked like it was from a hundred years ago, old people's furniture, faded and worn, the only thing shiny the frames of the pictures on the piano. A piano—what did she need that for? He took a step into the room and stopped, sniffing the air—pills, old clothes, dust. His throat contracted. He took a miniature Hershey bar from the bowl and put it in his pocket.

He slid open the drawer of a desk in the corner and ran his hand through the contents—bills, snapshots, store receipts. He pulled out a letter and read it: "Dear Sonia, I don't know if you heard about Eddie. He's gone from the cancer, but it was quick at the end." Rudy imagined himself an old man, sitting in a chair, his hands empty. He wouldn't wait for it like that, he thought. He slipped across the rug, his feet noiseless and went to stand in the hall, looking up the dark stairs. All quiet, he thought. To his left he could see into the kitchen where the light was on over the sink. Old people sometimes hid things in the freezer, he'd heard. He could see some tomatoes on the table, one of them leaking juice. He breathed in deeply—he'd just check out the dining room and then leave. In the dish cabinet, the rows of plates and glasses gleamed and winked.

He stepped in and halted, his breath coming fast. Someone was standing on the other side of the table—the old woman, her hair hanging down like a veil,. "I was just—" he said, "I was going to—" His ears roared as if they were filling up with blood.

Her eyes were fixed on him, but she hadn't moved. She stood with her hand on the table, moving it over the tablecloth, smoothing it over and over, her eyes wide open and milky blue, her skin almost gray. He could hear the tiny rasp of her fingers on the cloth, and her breathing, which was clotted and heavy. Rudy put one foot behind him, as if he could back away, each step moving him away from now. But Mrs. Knapik was moving at last. Her arm bent, her head rolled back, her hand clawed at the table, taking the cloth with it, and even as Rudy jumped forward, she hit the floor. Christ, Rudy thought, as he tried to untangle her arms from the tablecloth. Her head lay awkwardly against the table leg, the eyes closed at last, and he lifted it, feeling the bone of her skull against his palm, the faint warmth of her skin under her thin hair.

Ellie stood in front of the full length mirror in the hall. She had assembled the pieces of her uniform as quietly as she could, so Rudy wouldn't hear her. He had the television on downstairs, a baseball game. She turned so she could see how the skirt looked in the back. It would be nice if it was a different color—pink, maybe, or golden. Why couldn't a uniform look as nice as a bridesmaid dress? The pleats banged against her legs.

"Hi, I'm Ellie," she whispered to the mirror. She smoothed her hair, tangled from lying in bed. She went into her mother's room and got a purse out of the closet and went to stand in front of the mirror again. Her bare feet looked wrong, so she went to her room and got her old school shoes and put them on without socks, left them unlaced for comfort.

"Hi, I'm Ellie," she said again, holding the purse in front of her. She knew the way to the new school—up one block, through the parking lot of the police station, then another three blocks. She'd be walking all by herself. The nuns were supposed to be mean. They were the bride of Christ, but they couldn't have any children of their own. Ellie put out her hip and wagged her finger at her reflection. "I'm having Todd's baby," she said, "and I don't care who knows it."

Yawning, she sat down on the floor where she could still see herself in the mirror. She heard a noise and started to get up, but it wasn't Rudy, it wasn't inside the house. Holding the purse in front of her, she made a face at her reflection. "I'm perfectly fine, thank you." Outside she could hear a siren. The sound rose and belled until it seemed to be right under the stair window but she was too tired to go and look. Ellie lay down on the carpet with Dove's purse for a pillow and went to sleep, waves of red light coming through the window and washing over her. She dreamed that she heard someone talking, someone crying out. Her mother was singing, her father stood in the door of his cabin listening.

READING MARLEY

This was the period in my life when a fairly small propeller airplane, probably a Cessna 150, flew low over Old Brooklyn every night between eleven-thirty and twelve midnight. My house was always crowded with my friends, my brother's friends, people who wanted to see my mother after her stay in the hospital, hangers-on who wanted a place to stay or a free meal or just an ear, which is what I was to a lot of people then. So I was always up when this plane flew over. Eleven-thirty or twelve was early to me at that time, when I stayed awake until three usually, so I would hear it and wonder if Marley was at home hearing it as well. And then I was always glad for a little while that there were five or fifteen people between me and this thought, that I was making spaghetti for someone's late supper, that my mother was sitting at the kitchen table telling how they had to wrestle her down to give her a shot, that I was listening to my girlfriend, Pat.

Pat might be telling me how she had been conned into dealing with these children, her boyfriend's. Two little girls, watery pale blondes, noses running, wearing too-long, too-fancy dresses and tiny running shoes. She made them breakfast, found them day care, bought them socks and Wonder Woman underpants, rented kid movies for them. But when he dumped her, Pat missed those little girls, the feel of their smooth hair she had brushed and braided, the noises they made eating their cereal. She was a mess, drinking wine on the couch and talking about getting custody or kidnapping or just moving to California to get away – crazy talk.

Back and forth I went, to the kitchen to stir the spaghetti sauce, thick, red, spitting, which my mother was too intent on her own story to notice, back to the front room to take a sip out of Pat's glass. Oh, them interns aren't so smart as they'd like you to believe, my mother would say. Ask Lee Anne, she's had to deal with them plenty, haven't you, hon? Yes, I said, and yes to Pat, yes, yes, I'm here, I'm listening. Still, it seemed I had plenty of time to think of Marley.

He didn't like the plane. I didn't mind it myself except in that it reminded me of Marley, which sometimes depressed me or made me mad. But he didn't like it at all. He'd told me how he would be lying awake every night, hearing it and imagining it falling out of the sky, thinking that it was buzzing so low that the pilot could not climb, that it was piercing the roof of his third-floor bedroom. And so when I heard it, I would think of him lying in his bed, and often this was more than I could stand, thinking of Marley in bed, alone or not.

I'd had lots of advice on the subject of Marley. Mostly it was to the effect of – are you nuts? Forget about him, is what they said, Pat, my brother, my brother's biker friends, the biker friends' chicks, my unmarried pregnant cousin, the lady next door, all of them. My mother liked Marley because he always brought her a present when he visited. He had done that ever since he was a kid, when he spent more time at our house than his own. But even she would shake her head when the subject of Marley and me came up. She wouldn't say anything against him, but she'd shake her head in this way that indicated disappointment, not so much in him as at my foolishness.

And it wasn't as if I didn't know they were right. I knew that Marley couldn't be depended on. But it was this very undependability that kept me hanging on, for sometimes he'd be so nice, so deep. We'd sit on the couch or on the porch glider for hours, talking, and he'd tell me every single thing he was thinking. And I'd have it in my mind that I was really good for him, that I was helping him, that there was no one who could be for him what I was. I was proud that he always came to me when he was in trouble, when he was lowdown depressed.

All that went on for a long time. Mom would be in the hospital or out of it. My brother would be off his medication and ripping the phone out of the wall and alphabetizing the stuff in the medicine cabinet. Or he'd be taking the pills all right and apologizing to everyone he'd hurt or annoyed, the marks of anger fading from his face and body – the bruises and cuts, the black eyes. Pat would be over talking about those kids, or after a while about her new boyfriend, childless this one, but married. The next-door lady would be coming over just to see what was going on and to complain about the marks the bikes made in her lawn, especially when they fell over as they did sometimes when Pirate or Donny or Montana were drunk enough to forget about their kickstands.

Sometimes Marley was coming around – everybody's friend – drinking beer in front of the TV, candy for Mom, slapping the bikers on the back and flirting with their girls. And he'd give me a special look every once in a while as if to say we knew something, as if we were saving something for later. And so I kept waiting. Sometimes there was a little kissing, late, when the house was quiet. Sometimes we screwed upstairs in my single bed. Or we'd just go down by the lake and sit in the dark listening to the noise the water made.

Then at times he'd be there in a needy way. For days or weeks he couldn't stand to see anybody but me. He had stuff in his head that he had to empty out. People were following him people wanted him dead. The girl he'd been seeing was in league with these people, he said. He'd seen men hanging out on his street corner and the same men had come into the garage where he worked. We went over and over it until all the blackness was washed out of it, like a litany I'd take him through looking for logic and comfort. He'd eat the macaroni or meatloaf or whatever and then allow his head to rest against my palm, my fingers against his cheek.

And then for a while, months maybe, he'd be gone. We'd hear things, that he was with a girl who'd gone to high school with my brother, or that he had a new job in a factory making double minimum wage, or that he'd moved to Sandusky. During these months, he'd come by every once in a while, but never when I was there. He'd come by to see Mom – my best girl, he'd call her. Say hi to Lee Anne, he'd say.

During these times when he wasn't around I'd go and see his mother. She liked to talk about him, sometimes to brag, sometimes to complain. It was one of her things that he'd been misunderstood some-how, somewhere – not by her. Some teacher or friend or boss or his long-gone father had not seen what he was, had underestimated him or misjudged him, and now it was too late. She knew that if they had paid more attention to him when he was young he would have been different and would have had a different life. He was good at math and physics – concepts about space and time were an open book to him, she said. But he had always made stupid mistakes, adding or subtracting things wrong, or writing down the wrong number. He was too easily distracted from what he was doing, his mind humming with the correct pitching technique or what there was to eat for a snack at home or the buzz and whisper of the students sitting behind him. If it wasn't for this, she thought, he could have been something big in science, maybe almost next to Einstein. She would make me cups of tea and I would eat stale crumbling Oreos from her cookie jar, and then I would go home, leaving her sighing in her slippers and apron.

And all the while, I'd be going to my job and moving files from one drawer to another, and I'd be having long phone conversations with Pat and my mother and the women at work who hated their husbands, and I'd be opening the door to let in Mom's friends from bingo and Donny and Montana and their girlfriends, and I'd be cleaning up the plaster from where my brother had put his fist through the wall, and *still* I'd have too much time to think about Marley.

It was a sad life, but I didn't know it.

Now, I am married, two children, pregnant again, no day-care problems, a house with a bay window and a mantel to put Christmas cards on – not ours, rented, but who cares. Married. Pretty happy. Not to Marley, nor to anyone I knew then. I stepped out of that old life to get to this place.

What happened is this. Number one, I turned twenty-eight. I don't know why this seemed so much older than twenty-seven, but it did. I started having dreams where there were a hundred rooms I had to go through, all the same. I sat around a lot, not doing anything, not even thinking, but noticing things maybe, like the fact that one of my legs was shorter than the other. I began counting things, cars that went by while I was sitting on the porch, the squares of the sidewalk on the way to the bus stop, the number of times my boss went to the john before lunch.

Number two, Pat got back with her old boyfriend, the father of the two little girls, against all advice, and he celebrated their first-month anniversary by beating her up and dumping her again.

Number three, Mom sold the house to a fast food chain and put a down payment on a one-bedroom condominium.

This was all in a period when Marley was not coming around at all, the dead depressing part of winter. I said to myself, what am I going to do, get an apartment and set myself up as everybody's friend on a smaller scale? Will Marley still go to see Mom? How will I know if he said to say hi to Le Anne? My brother was out of it then, taking his medication in the VA hospital, quiet and white when I visited him there, like a fixture or a piece of furniture. Everything was changing.

So I dyed my hair blonde and made up my mind that it was over with Marley and me. I said so to anyone who was around. When I heard the plane buzzing overhead, I hummed a song from the radio. I bought a lot of frozen dinners. I signed up to join a bowling team. But all this was really still loving and thinking about Marley, because what was in the back of my mind was that he would hear about this, about my hair, about the house soon to be sold. He would hear that I wasn't feeding anybody spaghetti and that I didn't care anymore. And when he heard he would come around and he would see me – a new person. I saw myself opening the door of my future apartment to him. I saw us sitting on a new couch. I saw myself in a new nightgown watching him come toward me across the room, not drunk, not desperate.

So all that was still about Marley. And whether or not he heard anything or thought anything, I don't know.

And then while I was still thinking these Marley thoughts, Donny and Pirate came over and told me that Montana and his girl had broken up and that he was pretty low I bristled up a little since it sounded like an invitation to get out the spaghetti pot and sympathy, but it turned out that while Montana did want sympathy, he was willing to spring for dinner. He wanted to bend my ear at the Chinese restaurant over on Detroit Avenue – the sky was the limit. At first I said no, because wasn't I starting a new life? But the habit of being there, of listening, was hard to break, and so I said yes. And also, I had it in my mind that even though I knew it wasn't a date, it had certain of the appearances of a date, and that if Marley heard about it, it might sound like a date to him.

The weird thing is that when the night came to go to dinner, Saturday it was, Marley came over. I was ready half an hour early, so it was me opened the door for Marley, who looked surprised. This must have been one of the visits where he expected to see only Mom. But he came in and we all, Mom and Marley and I, sat down in the kitchen and I made coffee. There were some sugar cookies, so I put them out. And I cut some cake that was in the fridge. Marley had brought some tomatoes for Mom that his mother had put up from her garden and I took the jars from him and put them in the cupboard. Marley asked about selling the house and Mom told him all about it. He said he was thinking of moving to Cincinnati or Columbus where job opportunities seemed better. Mom said how her angina seemed to be tolerable but her back and her shoulders were worse and how she was thinking of seeing a chiropractor. He asked how I was. I said I was going out that night with Montana. I hadn't meant to say it just like that, but if I waited for Mom to mention it I'd wait all night. He didn't say anything to that though.

At seven-fifty Montana called and said he was running late and he would pick me up at eight-thirty instead of eight. I said OK and Marley stayed and stayed, eating up all the cookies, and then starting on the cake.

Around eight-twenty Montana called again and said how about if we went to the Italian place which is right down the street to save time since he was so late. I said OK. Marley said I bet he's standing you up.

And then it was eight-thirty and then eight-forty-five and there I was sitting around in my good pants and Pat's necklace. I sat there drinking my fifth cup of coffee and eating a slice of the cake from sheer irritation at Marley and Mom who were having this conversation on Scientology and Christian Science. Mom knew a nurse, she said, who was a Christian Scientist, which she personally could never understand. Marley asked if we had any salami. I brought him out some pepper cheese.

Finally, at nine-fifteen Montana showed up and apologized and we went out, Mom calling out to have a good time, Marley not saying anything.

We got in his car, but another car had pulled across the driveway and we couldn't back out. It was Montana's girlfriend, Rosalie, and she wanted to know what he thought he was doing, and who he was doing it with. So he said it was just Lee Anne, and she said, Ha, and he brought her over to the car window to see that it was me and she said, Oh well, that's OK then. Hi, I said. And she moved her car and we went out to dinner, where Montana talked the whole time about Rosalie and how much fun they had had riding together and how she would lay her head against his shoulder when they were on the bike and sing into his ear. "Born to be Wild" she would sing, and "Margaritaville." Which was pretty much what I'd expected out of dinner, except for the singing, which was a surprise. I'd never heard Rosalie sing a note.

When we came back, Marley's car was still there, he was still visiting with Mom. So I asked Montana if he wanted to sit in the car for a while and he pulled it around and turned the lights off. Montana told me how Rosalie had been the only woman with whom he could come with any consistency and how she was a bitch in the morning but by dinner was always telling jokes and stories, some of which he told me. We stayed there until I heard Marley leave.

Montana got out to walk me to the front door and when we got around to the porch we saw that there were words written in the snow. I opened the front door and turned on the porch light to see them better. Most of them were unreadable, just lines and curves. But one was clearer. It was in a smooth place where no one had walked and the letters were deep in the snow. There was a little tail to the last letter where whoever had written it had pulled his finger away. What does that look like, I said to Montana. Looks like it says whore, he said.

Might have been Rosalie, he said. Don't take it personal, Lee Anne. I said to him that certainly I didn't. But I did, because I knew that it must have been Marley, and I felt excited and horrified. Whore. I kept reading it in the snow. I went inside after a while and Montana went home. I sat on the couch in the dark and thought about it for a while. Was I mad? Yes, I was. But also I was sort of excited. Not to be called a whore, but at the effort. Marley had never taken me seriously before. What would I say when I saw him again? What I said would be very important, I thought, would have everything to do with our future relationship, if we had one at all. I repeated these words to myself: If we even had one at all. Finally I went upstairs to sleep.

When I woke up the next day I remembered instantly what I had seen in the snow, and I thought how strange it was that Marley would do something like that, and how this strangeness meant that he was beginning to be different. I walked around with these thoughts, carrying them with me while I made orange juice for my mother and helped her pack up a basket to take to my brother at the VA.

Just before lunch Montana called. I found out who it was that wrote that in the snow, he said. You don't have to worry about Rosalie. It was Donny and Pirate, he said. High as kites. It seemed they wanted to find out how it went with us and they came and hung around for a while but they got cold and they didn't want to talk to Mom when they were so drunk nor did they have any paper to leave a note and so they had written in the snow: We were here, where were you? Where, Montana said, not whore. I thought I'd let you know it wasn't whore and it wasn't Rosalie or anyone else laying something like that on you.

Well, thanks, Montana, I said. I'm feeling better already this fine day to hear about their incompetent note writing. Say what? Montana said. And then I hung up the phone and laughed until my nose ran.

That was it – the final thing that led me into my new life. I'd been looking for signs and waiting for unchangeable things to change for too long. No matter how I read them, they said the same thing. The sky, the snow, the birds on the fence, my brother's biker friends, they all said it. It was that Marley was not everywhere in my life and finally I knew it.

IN WILL'S ROOM

A month ago, Will was sleeping in his room with his girlfriend, their faces close to the floor on the thinness of a single mattress, hands trailing over the edge, fingers dipping to the coldness of the bare floor. It was night, and she crept up through the darkness of the house to him and while his parents slept, cocooned in the new addition, they sighed and touched in this attic room. Will's animals, the elk, the bear, the eagle, and the fox, looked down from the slanting ceiling, crouched in their leafy squares, their edges ruffled by the layers of warm air that live under the roof, always softening, always cooling, always descending. Before they slept, Will explained to her each book, each coverlet, the ancient camera, the handful of brown clay that holds the touch of his seven-year-old fingers, hardened now, the edges chipped. In a soft voice, he named them for her and set them aside.

Now, on the plane, flying through layers of air and cloud, Will is drowsing toward Sweden, a half-empty glass by his hand, which lies twitching on the tray. The flight attendant passes smiling, for his youth, for his nearly shaven head, for his red lips. She remembers how he lifted the old woman's folded coat overhead as if it were an offering, the old woman's eyes following his hands, troubled even as she framed her thanks. Would she be able to get it down again? Could she again ask this nice boy whose name she doesn't know? Can she hold his attention that long? Will he remember her or her coat, which is gray, like a lamb, gray and old and soft? She doesn't know his name: Will, who is going to Sweden where he will know no one and no thing. He has left his Learn Swedish tapes on a small table by the couch in his parents' home. He can say hello. He can ask for the toilet. When he left the house someone was sleeping in his room, slotted into the space of his bed – his mother's friend, her cheek on his pillow and her disordered hair, gray at the roots, her body wrapped in his sheets. On the plane, his head is nodding, he is dreaming of the animals in his room. They have come down from their prisons, down from the wall. The elk drops his head, pawing, shy. The bear is clumsy, the eagle clears his feathered throat. Only the fox steps up, vivid, flame-colored, eyes like topaz. Will will tell their fortunes, he holds the cards in his hand like a fan. His fingers twitch on the airline tray – smooth, featureless, gray – his eyelids twitch, his head is thrown back, throat exposed. The flight attendant is tender as she passes, hurrying to get more snacks. The old woman across the aisle is worried: his neck will hurt when he wakes, his neck will be stiff. He will not be able to reach up so easily to get her coat. He will be in pain, angry. He will avoid her eye. Her coat, like a blanket in its softness, warm as a pet animal, will be out of her reach. Will's eyeballs move under the lids as he speaks to the eagle and the fox, as he turns to face the elk and the bear. Toward each of them he holds out a card which is all they can know, for now.

Here is how to work the fan. Here is the closet – plenty of room. Here the bed, here the reading lamp, the jelly glass of wild flowers, small stack of towel and wash cloth. Yes, the woman says, yes, Will's mother's friend, the inheritor of Will's room for a week. Alone, she drops her bags and stands, bathed in the heated layers of the air, attic air, close, breathless, comforting. She goes to look at the pictures on the wall, but she is too tired to pay attention to them. She puts her books on Will's desk, moving out of the way an unframed picture of his sister at the prom, her dress gleaming, her hair curving around her cheeks. The picture is curling up at the edges and the woman presses it down, smoothing it with her fingers, smoothing it flat. She puts her clothes in Will's closet where his too-small clothes hang, stiff with disuse, the shoulders of the shirts like knives along the hangers' edges. The room seems brown to her, sepia like the photograph of a room where someone lived fifty years ago, someone whose hair and smile are anachronistic, someone whose voice is on a record. Before she goes down to dinner she picks up the lump of clay, fitting her fingers to its ridges and wondering what it is.

That night, she lies on the mattress tucked under the eaves, her face on Will's pillow where she tries, sleeping, to enter his dreams. Asleep, she can feel her separation from the rest of the house. Will's room: the air is Will's air, blowing across her in the restless stream of the fan. Will's animals look down on her. Will's clothes, hardened and crisped by their abandonment, shift and whisper in the closet. Downstairs, in the new addition, Will's parents and his sister sleep, but up here is another level of existence – the plane of Will, where the animals and the much-read books, the finger-ridged clay all live in the currents of the fan, like vegetables in the thick soup of the air.

Dreaming, she knows Will to be gone, for she has seen him, slender, graceful, and his belongings in piles – the balls of wool socks, the spill of books – slowly migrating into bags and moving out the door. He is on the plane to Sweden. But her cheek is on his pillow, his sheets enfold her, his animals are watching her sleep. She is a part of their fortune – the fortune Will dreams that he must tell them, but he doesn't know what to say about her, for she is his mother's friend. She is old.

On the eve of his departure, Will went to buy t-shirts, to buy ice cream. He listened graciously to a record a quarter of a century old that his mother and his mother's friend said he would love. He ate cookies from a plate, taking the last one. He slept on the couch, for his mother's friend was in his bed. When she got up in the morning, he would be gone. He will be gone.

The plane is silver against the sky, a bullet, a bird, a toy spun on a string of gravity, and inside the flight attendant wields her little cart, clanking down the aisle. Will is almost awake, his eyes are half open. Partly, he thinks that the elk, speaking to him so earnestly, wearing a wool sock on one of his forefeet, is on the plane with him, perhaps in the seat beside him. Partly, he believes himself to be asleep, his cheek on the worn-smooth linen of his pillow, his hand just touching the cool linoleum. And partly, he knows himself to be on his way to Sweden – he can see with half of one of his eyes the curving hip of the flight attendant as she backs down the aisle toward him, her uniform sky blue and smooth. It is morning, his head and his arms are empty. His room, a thousand miles away, is closing in on itself, a puzzle from which pieces have been lost. As the woman, his mother's friend, is sleeping, the sheet thrown back to show her throat, the walls are shrugging closer, the ceiling bends like a bow. But Will is moving through layers of air, each thick with molecules like raisins in a cake, the plane a little silver knife to cut them through.

COMPANY

Grace tapped her fingers against the ashtray sitting next to her on the couch. Before her wedding six months ago, people had given her things like a pewter coffee set, and delicate footed mugs with matching plates—the kind of thing that her mother and the other older women who had chosen them expected she would use when people came visiting. She imagined that they had thought of her pouring coffee from the pewter coffee pot and cutting homemade cake to put on the flowered plates.

"Do you want another hit?" Jimmy asked her.

"Mmhmm," she said. He had come over to hang out with Sean, who wasn't here. He had hardly seemed to listen when she explained that Sean was at the park three blocks away, playing basketball with some guys he knew from high school. Jimmy's eyes were glassy and wide. He was high, she knew, but it didn't bother her. Jimmy was always cool. He never got weird or crazy.

They were sitting on the ancient sectional sofa she had gotten at a garage sale. Some time long ago in the past it must have been in fashion, although it was hard to believe that anyone had ever wanted a brown upholstered monster with scratchy gold threads in a maddening pattern. Jimmy was sprawled at one end and she sat at the other, her legs drawn up, her chin resting on her knees. He leaned forward to pass her the joint they were sharing.

"Sean is..." he paused while she inhaled, but then didn't go on.

"Playing basketball?" she said, holding her breath and the smoke in. Her words squeaked out. In a few minutes she would find that unbearably funny, but now she felt embarrassed.

"Basketball," Jimmy said. "He always liked that kind of thing."

"I can give him a message," Grace said. "If he doesn't come back."

He looked at her gravely, and she felt as if what she'd said had some kind of importance that she didn't realize. "I thought we'd all go the Picadilly," Jimmy said slowly. She'd passed the joint back to him and he held it consideringly between thumb and finger. "I'm going to roadie for Dragonwyck, and I can bring along anyone I want." He inhaled, held it, then let the smoke trickle out. "For free," he added. He leaned forward to pass the joint back, and rested one hand on her leg, balancing.

The touch of his hand was surprising to her. She looked down at it, darker than her very fair skin. She could never get a tan, no matter how she tried. Her mother said it was just as well, since tanning made for wrinkles, but her legs looked sick in summer, white, like the underside of a fish. She took the joint and pushed at Jimmy so that he moved back.

"You ever been there?" he asked.

"Where?" she said.

"The Picadilly."

"No. Is it nice?"

"It's a dive." He laughed. "That's why we love it."

Who was we, she wondered.

He leaned forward again, and she tensed, thinking he would touch her again. "You going to take a hit or what?"

Grace had forgotten about the joint. She barely sipped at it, for she could feel the cloudy heaviness beginning to fill her head, and passed it back. It was so short now that his fingers were close to its burning end. He pinched it knowingly and inhaled, his teeth showing.

She wished that Sean would come back, although she was mad at him. He hadn't wanted to go to the mall with her, or to the coffee house, or to the park, or in fact anywhere at all with her. Do you think you're still in high school, she'd yelled at him. Because you're not. You're a married man. She didn't like to think of the ugly look that had come over his face when she said that, as if he hated the sound of it. It's not as if I like being married all that much, she thought now. The beginning part was fun, the sex, and sleeping in the same bed. But the rest. She rubbed the bare soles of her feet against the scratchy couch, which seemed to wake nerves in her body she hadn't known about. Jimmy had laid his head against the back of the couch and was staring at the ceiling.

"Let's go outside," Jimmy said.

"It's getting dark," she said.

"No, no," he said, shaking his head. He got up, barely stumbling. "This high needs room to expand. We have to be outside for this one."

"Why?" she said, but he didn't answer, and when he held out his hand, she took it. He pulled her to her feet in a smooth move that made her feel as if she had thinned and lightened, as if her bones were filling with air.

They went through the house without turning on the lights, and out the back door. The uncut grass brushed against her ankles and made her itch, but the itch seemed wonderful, a luscious abrasion that made her skin start to burn. The backyard was darker than the street and she and Jimmy melted into the shadows. There were two lawn chairs, one overturned, but Jimmy passed them and led her to the square of grass that was bounded by the chainlink fence and two garages, one belonging to the old woman next door. The grass here was even longer, and when Jimmy sank down into it, pulling her with him, it brushed against her ankles. Jimmy let go of her hand. She had felt silly and childish when he was pulling her across the yard, but now she felt untethered, as if her lightness would become a serious liability. If there were a wind, she might blow along the ground, she thought, like a plastic bag from the grocery store belled out into a sail.

Jimmy stubbed the joint they'd finished into the dirt, scraping back the grass to make a place for it. He tore off grass and dandelion leaves and laid them over the joint. "In nomine patri, ..." He lit another joint he pulled from his shirt pocket and handed it to her. "I used to be an altar boy," he said. When Grace took it and put it between her lips, he said, "This is my body, this is my blood."

"That's perverted," she said, and took a good long drag. Out here in the near dark, she felt better than she had in the house, but she was glad that they were back by the garage, more or less out of sight. The old woman who lived next door was always spying. She kept coming over and bringing cookies, but she never stopped looking around when she was in the house, snooping. She asked questions about how often Grace did the dishes, and if she waxed the floor or only mopped.

"I'll never wax a floor," she said to Jimmy. "I won't do it."

"That's cool," he said. "So, do you want to go?"

"Go where?" She could see the old woman's kitchen window from here, a yellow square of light. The old woman crossed the square, carrying something. A plate with something on it. Maybe cake. Maybe she had company. We both have company, she thought, which was funny. It was very funny, really.

"The Picadilly."

"Sean's not back yet." She watched the old woman cross back and forth, carrying things that she couldn't quite see.

"If you come, you can meet Jojo. He's the lead singer."

"I know," she said, although she had no idea who he was.

"All the girls like him."

"I know, I know."

"He's got charisma, which is a pretty cool word, don't you think?"

She crossed her legs and sat up primly. "I don't like him." Her head felt remarkably steady, its balance on her shoulders something to be admired.

"You don't?" Jimmy rolled over on his side, as if he wanted to see her face.

"I don't like him at all."

"Who do you like?" His voice was very quiet. There was no wind and his voice was a small thing in the dark air.

She looked at him, squinting a little. "This is silly," she said.

"Not as silly as some things," Jimmy said. "Some things are so silly I can't hardly stand it. Like politics. If you want to talk about silly." He moved a little nearer.

The joint was burning in her fingers, and she took an absent-minded drag. Jimmy's hair fell over the arm he had his head propped on, so long that it trailed in the grass, or probably did. It was too dark to be sure.

"The dog next door is silly," Grace said. "My neighbor's dog. He's, you know, a poodle," she made circles in the air with her hands, "all poofy and curly." She began to laugh, and Jimmy laughed, too. "He wears a bow." She put her hands over her mouth.

Jimmy laughed again. "What color?"

"Sssh," she said, "don't laugh." But she couldn't stop either.

"What color?" he said, moving closer.

"Stop, it's too funny," she said. They both laughed harder, taking gasping breaths, trying to stifle themselves. She firmed up her mouth and took a deep breath, held up one hand as if to say, wait. "Ok," she said, her laughter under control. "We have to be quiet. I mean it." She looked toward the neighbor's house. There were two people in the kitchen now, her neighbor and another old woman, arranged in the window looking toward each other as if they were in a painting. Their mouths were moving, but she couldn't tell if they were talking or chewing. This almost made her start laughing again, but she bit her lip so she wouldn't.

"Math is silly. No, it's stupid," Jimmy said. "School is stupid. I'm glad to be out of all that."

She nodded, although she had liked school, mostly. "House-work is stupid," she said.

" Doing dishes is the stupidest thing in the world. You have to do them every day."

Jimmy nodded at this truth. "Do you have any cookies? Like Oreos?"

"I don't know," she said. "I could go and look."

"No, don't go. It's no big."

The grass was warm and slightly damp. It was black now, all the color drained out of the shadows between the garages. The joint was done, and Jimmy buried it next to the first one, drifting bits of leaf over it with ceremonial care.

"Sean should be back soon," she said, although probably he wouldn't be. He always went to the Jigsaw for a beer after.

"Soon," Jimmy said, drawing the word out, "Soooooon. If we were out in the country, we'd be able to see the stars."

"I suppose," she said.

"The stars aren't stupid," Jimmy said.

"No," she said.

He had moved a little, turning his face to the light from her neighbor's window. Grace could see the bridge of his nose, and the high curve of his cheekbone. "You know what's totally stupid?" he said.

"What?" She didn't care really, but she was starting to feel odd, as if she had separated from herself, as if one part of her had drawn away and was looking at the other part with cold dislike.

Jimmy's head darted forward, and though the motion was quick, it seemed to take a long time, his hair falling forward, the little rustle of the grass as his body moved over it. She jerked back, thinking he was go-ing to take her arm, but instead he licked her knee, his tongue rough and warm. He lapped at it slowly, and she saw the glitter of his eye, watching her while he did it.

He lay back again, his eyes still on her. "Basketball," he said. "Basketball is the stupidest thing on earth."

Grace pulled both knees against her chest reflexively, circling them with her arms. Now she ought to get up, or invoke Sean's name. "I'm a married woman," she said, but this sounded so ridiculous that it made her laugh. She had a vision of herself in an old-fashioned dress saying this to someone holding a gun--something she'd seen in a movie, she realized, and thought herself very clever to have pinned this down.

"Marriage is stupid," Jimmy said.

Grace sighed. She hugged her knees more tightly.

Jimmy lay back down on the grass, his arms crossed behind his head. "The question is, should we or shouldn't we."

Grace squinted at him, trying to make out his face in the near dark. "I already said."

"I meant, roll another joint." He patted his shirt pocket. "I've got enough for one more."

Grace looked over at the next door window. Her neighbor was pouring something from a green teapot into a matching cup that her guest held out to her. She felt a space inside herself that she hadn't noticed before, a space that Jimmy had somehow shown her. "I don't care," she said.

"Should I or shouldn't I waste a perfectly good jay on someone who doesn't care." Jimmy was holding out a bag of weed on the palm of his hand as if he were balancing it on scales.

Grace would have liked to get up and walk away, but her knees and in fact all her joints felt disconnected. It would be embarrassing to fall, to have Jimmy see her fall and try to get up. She'd always been clumsy, as her mother had often pointed out to her. She could hear her mother's voice saying it--you've always been clumsy, and you should have known better than to smoke that awful stuff.

"I'm going to take that as a yes." Jimmy deftly rolled the cigarette paper into a neat tube, tucked in at both ends. "I say we should smoke this and then..." he let his voice trail off.

"Then what?" Grace asked. She could hear the phone ringing inside the house, her phone, her house. Who would it be? Her mother. Sean, saying he was bringing back some pizza. Ginny who maybe wanted to come over and hang out. It might be good if Ginny came over, because she could talk to Jimmy, and to Grace's mother if she showed up. Sean would not be coming with pizza. He was at the Jigsaw right now with a beer in front of him watching one of his stupid friends pretend he knew how to play pool.

"Then you can decide whether you want to blow me or not," Jimmy said. He handed her the joint. "Just kidding."

"Where did you meet Sean?" Grace took the joint. Her lips were wet and the paper stuck when she drew in.

"Sean and my brother went to high school together. They were on the football team." He shot her with his finger. "Football is stupid. You know that, right?"

"I don't know," Grace said. "I don't know anything."

"Listen to me then," Jimmy said. He sat up and put his face close to hers. "Listen to me, and I'll tell you. Whatever you want to know."

"I don't know what I want to know," Grace said.

"Neither do I," Jimmy said. "That's what makes it so perfect." He leaned in, and she watched his features grow sharper. His eyes had a wet shine, his mouth looked soft, half hidden in the careless growth of his beard. His hair was longer than hers, which would make her mother frown in distaste. It fell forward as he moved against her and she could feel it touching her arms where they were bare below the short sleeves of her t-shirt.

Jimmy put his mouth on hers, rubbing it as if he was asking a question. As if she were a lamp, Grace thought, and he was Aladdin. How stupid she was, to be thinking of such a thing. Why couldn't she be thinking of something romantic, why couldn't she be a princess or an actress. Why couldn't there be a candle or--- she didn't know, but--

"Kiss me for real," Jimmy said. "Do I have to do all the work?"

Grace put a hand up and found his hair. She took a handful and pulled it, but didn't move her mouth away. They were both leaning forward, their bodies otherwise untouching. "Maybe I don't want to kiss you," she said, but she didn't move away.

Jimmy put his fingers on her lips and pulled at the lower one a little. "Come on, Gracie. Come on."

"Kissing is stupid," Grace said. She opened her mouth a little, and he sucked on her tongue.

"No, it isn't." Jimmy's voice was muffled, his mouth moving on hers, burrowing inside.

Grace's eyes were open—it seemed wrong to close them and abandon herself to this entirely. She could see the side of her neighbor's garage past Jimmy's shoulder, dark with a slash of light from the street-light that revealed the peeling paint in harsh relief. Her neighbor had a car but she never drove it. It had belonged to her husband, who was dead. She didn't know how to drive. How could she stand not knowing how to drive? Her son would come once a week and drive her in the car to grocery shop. What kind of a life was that?

Jimmy reached forward and put his hands on her shoulders, pulling her toward and under him a little, and Grace let herself be moved. His flannel shirt was unbuttoned, and she could feel his skin against hers above the neck of her shirt. He took his mouth away from hers for a minute. "Jesus, Grace," he said. He nuzzled against her neck, pushing inside her collar. He held her shoulder with one hand, and with the other began to pull at the waistband of her shorts.

Grace let her head fall back. She was thinking about Sean, how she'd met him at Ginny's. He had looked at her from across Ginny's basement for a long time before he came over. Jimmy's hand was fumbling at the button of her shorts and she wiggled a little in a way that might have meant she wanted him to get off, but she knew it didn't mean that at all. Jimmy slid his hand into her bra and panted against her neck. "What about the Picadilly," Grace said, her mouth against his ear.

"The Picadilly is stupid," Jimmy said.

"Wait," Grace said. "I mean it."

Jimmy stopped moving. He lay half across her, one hand in her shirt, the other underneath her, almost inside her shorts. "Grace," he said. "Gracie Grace."

"I don't want to--" Grace said, but he interrupted her, moving his mouth against the skin of her chest.

"You don't want to go to the Picadilly," he said. "I'm telling you that so you'll know it."

Grace's shoulders twitched. She felt as if she were sinking into the grass. She could feel its dampness working its way into her clothes. "What if I do want to go?"

Jimmy rolled away from her but kept his hands on her. "You don't. You know what goes on in the johns there?" He rubbed back and forth with just the tips of his fingers. "People getting it on every which way. Scoring drugs. There's something else for you to know."

Grace didn't answer. The sky was not black but a very dark blue, something she wouldn't have guessed. It was a color that had to be experienced to be known. "Would you like some coffee?" she asked.

"Coffee is stupid," Jimmy said. He bent over and pushed his mouth onto hers, and when she tried weakly to slide out from under him, he clamped her arms and held her down.

He only half undressed her, pulled her shorts and underwear down, and she let him, lifting her hips to help. All the while, and while he was pushing inside her, she kept her eyes open, watching the sky, and her neighbor's window, which shone yellow like a rectangular sun. Her neighbor's company was gone. Soon she would go to bed, for she didn't stay up much past ten. Soon, Grace said to herself. Soon Sean would come home, or he wouldn't.

JANE, DREAMING

This is all a dream. The woman dreaming it is lying in bed next to her lover, covered up except for her forehead and her left leg from the knee down. This is Jane, Jane who is dreaming, Jane who is saying, "May I have two of these?" at the same time that she is turning over in bed, her foot curling around her lover's calf, her hand finding the small of her lover's back.

"May I have two of these apples?" which are a hard, shiny red, nestled among the cards of buttons, red gleaming buttons, on the dollar store counter. "What lovely apples!" Jane says to the dime store clerk.

And how amazing, she thinks, that the dollar store is so exactly as it was when she was five: the pleasantly dusty wooden floors, the tiny plastic dolls with their pink flower lips identically pursed, the racks of aprons, the merchandise piled on the counters and stacked in the aisles and crawling up the walls to the high ceiling.

"How have you kept the ceiling so high?" Jane asks the clerk who is looking for a bag for the apples. He pauses, thinking, and Jane sees that he is beautiful, more beautiful than anyone she has ever known.

She leans across the counter and puts her hand on his chest, just touching his shirt, his beautiful white shirt. She is worried that some-one will come in. she can hear the old woman humming, the owner or manager, who is doing inventory in the back, but still she leans across the counter and hooks her fingers in the clerk's shirt front, between the second and third buttons, and pulls him forward. She knows his name. she knows that he has a sister whom he does not love, and that he likes to fuck in the water, to lie half submerged, his wet hair washing back and forth over his shoulders.

"I know where we can go," she says to him, breathing the words into his ear. She has moved around the counter and they are standing with their arms around each other. She can hear the old woman's humming, closer, moving down the aisles toward them, carrying something, dragging something. "Please," Jane says. "I know where there is water."

When they leave the store, she is so happy, she could be flying. The water is ahead of them, the little waves dancing, the light gleaming off them. She is taking off her shirt as they run down the street, each shiny red button falling to the ground as she unbuttons it, bouncing down the street behind them like cherries. The clerk is ahead of her, running in the shallows, pumping his bare legs high, great splashes rising with each leap.

"Wait," she calls after him. Although he is far out into the water, it is still shallow, it barely reaches his ankles. "Wait," Jane calls after him, "it's happening now." She clenches her hand on the last of her buttons, but there is nothing in it. Her nails dig into her palms and

Yawning, she straightens her fingers and tries to see the clock. She is so thirsty, but she is so tired. She pokes her lover a little to see if he will wake up, but he is sleeping heavily on his stomach, his head turned away from her. She closes her eyes experimentally: will she go to sleep? She believes that she can still see the room – the light block of the window, the dark bulks of furniture, the featureless squares that are picture on the wall – through her eyelids. She opens her eyes to check but the room looks wrong, the window is in the wrong place. Closed – better, the dark and light shapes are smoother, lovelier, they flow. Open: no, really not as nice. Closed. Open. Closed open

Closed. Jane has a new job, which she likes much better than her old job at the insurance company. Now she is doing PR for a rock band. They are all staying at a house, a big house, and they are going to

do some publicity pictures. Jane is wandering through all the rooms of
the house looking for props. In the cavernous dining room she finds a
pair of glass candlesticks, three-branched, one blue, one green. She holds
them up to the light.

These will look nice, she thinks, but a woman glides over and
takes them from Jane's hands, sets them on the table. Jane explains that
it is just for the pictures, but the woman shakes her head.

Jane is worried because she doesn't know who this woman is –
does she live here? Jane is worried because she doesn't want to lose her
job. She likes the drummer of the rock band especially, and she thinks
that they might be going to get married. They are going to get married
and have a baby. She can see, as if on a television, scenes from this life
reflected in the mirror on the dining room wall.

"I'm going to have red hair – look at that," she says to the woman. "I'm going to live by the sea." The woman is gliding away, beckoning
for Jane to follow, which she does, reluctantly. But she can't forget the
candlesticks, gleaming, transparent, the feel of them in her hand – knob-
by, the lumps of the carvings against her palm. As they go down the
hall, she looks back and she sees them glowing on the table, gleaming,
sliding, melting into the gloom, and she realizes that the carvings were
letters – a message, and she tries to turn back, but she can't, tries to turn
but she can't, tries, can't. She is gliding, sliding down the hall, the floor is
sliding her along, a conveyor belt, and the walls glide by, the portraits of
old women look out at her, the china vases on the tables wink and glitter
although it is dark. There are sparkles of light although it is dark. The
woman ahead of her beckons her on and the rings on her fingers twinkle,
although it is dark, dark.

And for a little while there is a space of dark, just the dark,
nothing else, dark fish gliding through dark water, the velvet dark where
you might imagine soft black sand sifting down grain by grain through
the dim waters. Dark ribbons of weed, dark flowers. Long waves of dark
sound, so long and slow they cannot be heard.

In the bedroom the moon lights the curtains. They glow white-
ly. On the dresser, two quarters and a dime shine silver against the dark
wood – money for parking. Jane's jeans lie in a tumble on the floor. The

alarm clock is set for 7, but she will not get up until 7:45. She will be late going back home. Her husband will have sent the children whining off to school. He will have left her a nasty note.

Her lover doesn't have to get up. He books dancers into clubs and probably does some other more unsavory things. Jane is jealous of the dancers, who are very young and sexy if not always beautiful. Jane is nice to them if they call or if she is out with her lover in the clubs. She admires their smooth skin and silky hair, their really tiny hips and flat stomachs.

Jane cannot remember when her own stomach was flat, although she knows it was, it must have been, before she had children. Before the first one, the little boy, her stomach must have been lovely, a smooth stretch of skin between the staunch bones of her hips. But she can't remember how it looked or how it felt. She puts her hand on her stomach now feeling the scar that makes a road from navel to pubic hair, the delicate webbing of symmetrically stretched skin.

She has asked her lover if he minds it, but he doesn't like to answer questions. He likes to party, drink and smoke and fuck. He likes to be moving whenever he's not asleep. He is always traveling, sometimes with Jane. Jane imagines that someday they will leave for good. She wants to live someplace else, maybe California. She wants to go to California, she wants to live in a beautiful house and go grocery

shopping in California – the palm trees are amazing, Jane thinks, tilting her head back. If only they didn't have to drive the ugly old dirty-white car that belongs to her husband, when the colors of everything else are so bright, shiny and almost pulsing with life. She and her lover are shopping. The store is a special California store with a different kind of music in each aisle. Strauss waltzes in dairy. Heavy metal by the meat case. Reggae in the double aisle of frozen foods.

We have to stay in California, she tells her lover, because this is so cool. He is trying to decide between frozen peas and frozen broccoli while the reggae musicians gather around them in a circle, bobbing and shaking their shoulders. Each item in their cart is a different color – a blue box of pasta, a silvery cylinder of juice, a yellow triangle of cheese, each more lovely than the one before. I can't wait for the kids to see this, Jane thinks, but she remembers they haven't come to California.

At the checkout counter, Jane starts to write a check, but the cashier says that her checks are wrong. Jane and her lover will have to talk to the manager. This is how it is done in California. The cashier takes them upstairs, where a tiny man in a white suit tells them they have to take a test before they can have their check cashed. There are test papers in front of them marked with their names.

Do you believe in God? the tiny man asks. What color is the soul? What did your mother say to your father when they met? What was the name of the little girl whose pixie-stick candy you stole in first grade. Jane and her lover are allowed to consult and she thinks they are doing pretty well.

Then the man leans forward and gestures to a round table at the side of the porch, which has cakes arranged on it around the edge. The last question is written on the cakes. He begins cutting pieces of the cakes and eating them, grinning, chewing with his mouth full.

"Stop," Jane begs him. His teeth are very white. Stop, she keeps telling him to stop, so she can answer the question, but he won't. Jane's lover has melted away and she starts to cry because she misses him, because they are not going to live in California, because the answer cakes are disappearing. The tiny man gives her the last piece, and it is spicy and fragrant, although she gets only the thinnest slice, or maybe she doesn't even get any of it at all, maybe she only imagines how it would taste, licking her lips, which are dry, she's thirsty

but she doesn't wake

and she is in her house, the house where she lives with her husband, but it is filled with water. The water is clear but with a greenish tinge. It is in some places only up to her waist, but in others chest- or shoulder-high. She wanders through the rooms looking at her furniture under the water and it is lovely, shimmery and slippery looking. The carpet is much softer, she thinks. The hems of the curtains waver slowly in the invisible currents that run through the water. The plants are floating about in little boats, at which she nods her head: yes, that makes sense. how the children will like that, she thinks, the little boy and the older girl.

She opens a door and sees the hallway that leads to the back of the house, where her children and her husband are, and here the water is higher. It reaches the ceiling. She can look into it as if it is a mirror, she can feel it pressing against her, bulging out through the doorway. She knows that she has to walk into it, she has to go down the hallway, which is filled with water to the ceiling, and she thinks she can't do it. But then she remembers that she used to be able to breathe under water when she was a child. All she has to do is remember how, and she holds herself stiff, her hands pressing against the bulging wall of water until it comes to her – the old way of breathing.

She walks into the water, which encloses her and enters through her nostrils and her mouth and flows all through her body. She walks down the hall, her familiar back hall, her body wavering and shimmering in the water

and – snap – she is awake, and for some reason she can't remember, she is afraid. She rolls over for the comfort of her lover's body, hoping he will wake up. "I dreamed I could breathe under water," she says, a little louder than a whisper, but he doesn't stir. She rolls to her back and lies there, rubbing her legs against the sheets, trying to remember what the dream was about: something about cake? About water? She is still a little frightened, so she keeps her eyes open. She doesn't want to fall back into the same frightening dream, whatever it was.

The room is darker than it ought to be. There are little swirls of light from the streetlight. She watches a patch of light that glows in the corner of the room, near the ceiling. What could be making it, she wonders. It is a wonderful pearly light, roundish but stretching down the wall. Jane feels that she loves it. It is as beautiful as a child, as one of her own children sleeping with her husband, who thinks she is at an insurance convention.

Her husband is on disability: a back injury. He is retraining for a position in computers at the community college. He is thinking of running for councilman since he has some spare time. He believes he has something to contribute. On his bedside table there is a copy of Stephen Hawking's book in which he was marking quotes to use in a speech he will give tomorrow at the Moose Lodge. He wants Jane to come out with him when he gives speeches, but she doesn't want to.

Jane wants to have more fun, she wants to lose five pounds. She wants her office mate to stop smoking in the restroom. She wants to know what happened to the earring she lost last week, she wants to have a better relationship with her mother, she wants her son to stop whining, her daughter to stop sucking her hair.

She lies still, looking at the light in the corner from behind her half-open lids. It bows and sways and shivers. It slides down the wall, following a line of flowers in the wallpaper, and suddenly Jane feels uneasy. It can't be a light from outside, she thinks. The light would have to be up in the branches of the eighty-foot silver maple outside the window. The light seems blobbier, more solid. It seems to be coming nearer and Jane is gripped by fear. She ought to do something, but she can't think what. She can only shut her eyes and lie, trembling, not even able to move her arm or leg to touch her lover for comfort. Is it coming nearer? If she opens her eyes will it be above her, bobbing and glowing

bobbing and glowing, bobbing glowing, there is a trail, a path and Jane follows it down to the sea. This is a dream about light. The sea is not water but light, rising in great soundless waves. There is no sun, but the sky is full of light which falls like rain. Jane stands on the beach, on the edge where the waves of light run up just short of her toes. The grains of sand under her feet are sparkling like tiny stars. Jane is breathing in light and she is very happy.

She is waiting for a boat to come over the light-water, and she thinks she sees it, far out, a tiny glowing, bobbing shape that is coming closer. When it gets here, she thinks, when it gets here… but she doesn't have any thoughts that describe what will happen. She can see it will take the boat a long time to reach her, and so she walks down the beach, dragging her feet through the sparkling sand.

Just ahead, she can see an old house, yellow-painted with green trim, her parents' house. She puts her hand on the front door and it swings open. She looks out over the water but the boat is still far out and she goes in. Here is the hall, the little table and the mirror. Here is the living room, just as it used to be, except that there is a card table in the middle of the floor, as if her mother might be having bridge club. Jane draws the drapes across.

Her daughter is sleeping on the couch, a piece of hair still in her mouth. Jane's former lover, a man she met at the hardware store, knocks on the door. Jane is excited to see him at first but she is afraid her daughter will wake up. He is fatter than she remembers. She is pushing him away as he tries to put his arms around her when a woman, an old woman comes through the house from the back. "I need directions," she says impatiently. Jane refuses to answer. She puts her arms around her exlover to distract him, to make him think she still loves him. The old woman is smiling. She goes to the cabinet in the dining room. All Jane's mother's china is in there, and as Jane watches, the woman takes out one of the gold and blue lusterware cups and balances it on her head.

"I can't stay," Jane says. Her daughter is moaning on the couch, breathing through her mouth, about to wake up, and Jane doesn't want her to wake up. She is so unhappy when she's awake. She cries, she's unpopular. Jane tries to pull the old woman out the door, and as she drags her out onto the porch, she sees her old front yard, the cushiony hydrangea bush, the bridal wreath. She sees her old street, the smooth red bricks, the mailbox on the corner. The sea of light is gone, the boat, the shining sand. She sinks down on the top step and begins to cry.

Across the street, a great silver plane is crashing and burning, each little flame as bright as the sun. Her old lover has come out on the porch, and he puts his hand on her breast

her new lover puts his hand on her breast, breathing into her ear and Jane turns toward him, rising up through layers of sleep. It is stickily warm under the blankets and, even half drowsing, Jane registers the familiar irritation – he doesn't keep his room cold enough for her. He likes it tropical. No need for blankets – they could sleep under a sheet or with nothing over their bodies. But her lover can't sleep that way. He likes it hot, he says. I'm a cold fish, he says, I'm a reptile.

The reptile is smoothing his hand down the length of her thigh, so slowly that she begins to sink again through the layers. His hand is on her breast, her navel, the tangle of her pubic hair, but even as she is opening her lips to him, even as her skin begin to tingle, she is falling asleep, asleep, sleep and she is in love. She lies in a small house, very clean and bright. No one comes there except for the man who is kissing her now. He is kissing her slowly, his tongue pushing gently between her lips, his hand sliding between her legs. She is naked, she is always naked in this house. The windows are always open. There are never any curtains. She walks naked through the house waiting for the man to come and make love to her. One hand holds the back of her neck and the hand is soft, something to lean her head against, but the hand between her legs is hard.

She leans her head back and it is as if she is floating in the clean bright air of the little house. When he enters her she opens her eye wide so that she can see all the colors of the house – they pierce her, one by one, turning like a wheel. When she comes it all goes dark.

When she climbs and crawls her way out of the dark, she is walking down an empty street lined with heaps of stuff, trash that hasn't been collected? But there is so much of it, the piles tower higher than her head. The streetlights are on although it is day. It is going to rain, it is going to rain soon. Bits of trash are blowing about in the rising wind.

There is going to be a storm, but Jane thinks she might find something pretty, something that has been thrown away by mistake – a ring, a velvet box, a treasure map. She picks up first one thing and then another and then she sees a glow at the bottom of one of the piles. She paws through old newspaper, animal bones, carpet remnants, and finds a picture, a picture of her mother when she was young. Her hair is black. She is wearing a light-colored dress. Her head is turned toward something outside the frame. It is glowing and as Jane looks at it she begins to hear a voice that she believes is from outside the dream. Your mother is dead, it says, your mother is dead, over and over. Yes, Jane thinks, she is dead.

Mother is dead, she thinks, waking. She can't remember the funeral. The wind is up outside. The blinds are rattling. Things are blowing around outside, and inside the room their small dark shadows are flitting about on the walls. The windows are loose, but her lover is not interested in caulking them or in any kind of home repairs. The house is one he inherited from his grandfather who would be shocked to see what happens there now, parties with drugs, beer for breakfast, and sex, sex all the time, morning noon night. It's too late, Jane thinks about her mother.

She remembers holding the picture of her mother in her hands and how it glowed. Did this happen at the funeral? But no, she remembers – it was a dream. There is still time to be nice, but Jane is so tired. She can't see the clock's green numbers. Her mother is not dead

but Jane is. Jane is dead. Jane is at the pool where she learned to swim when she was seven. She used to go herself, walking the five blocks, her bathing suit rolled up into a towel, some money in her little plastic purse for a candy bar after the lesson. She used to love her swimming teacher, used to pretend that the swimming teacher was her mother. Now Jane is dead, but she is not unhappy. Her eyes are open. She can't turn her head, though, because she is dead. She is sitting in a beautiful chair, a chair like a throne. She is naked, but she is wearing jewelry.

She is covered and wreathed and looped with jewels, her arms, her neck, her ankles, even her hair is braided with golden chains. She wishes she could raise her arm or her leg to admire how she looks so bedecked, but she can't move, because she is dead.

In front of her, the water in the pool ripples as if there is a wind rushing across it. The blue water rises in little peaks. Tiny whirlpools appear, no bigger than the palm of Jane's hand. As the invisible wind runs faster and harder over the surface of the water, Jane's chair begins to rise. She is dead and she is rising toward the ceiling, jewels dripping off her as she moves upward. The rubies, sapphires, pearls slide from her wrists, her fingers, her ankles. She can feel them gliding over her skin, although she is dead. She would raise her hands to save them if she could, but she is dead, and they fall away from her and slip into the water, among the tiny waves and whirlpools. By the light of the underwater lights, she can see them lying on the floor of the pool, glowing and winking. When she rises through the ceiling, she feels, although she is dead, joy and pleasure, better than sex, from the caress of the joists and beams and mortar of the building. I have to remember this, she thinks, I have to write this down, but she can't. She hasn't any paper and she can't move her arms because she is dead, and as she rises into the sky she begins to cry

and still crying, she tries to wake her lover. I had a bad dream, she says, very quietly, when he grunts but doesn't wake. She knows that he doesn't really love her. Her husband loves her, but his devotion is familiar. With tears drying on her cheeks, Jane lies awake, thinking about the next day. She has forgotten the dream, although her cheeks are still wet. The next day is Saturday and supposedly she will be returning from the conference. Her husband is scheduled to give a speech at a local PTA meeting, and she will go, out of guilt. She will take her daughter to her ballet class. She will call her mother to tell her she is coming to dinner on Sunday. They will fight as they always do, about whether Jane's daughter is too thin, about whether Jane's son should play peewee football, about the right way to make meatloaf, about Jane's husband who isn't, according to Jane's mother, trying hard enough to find a job.

Jane sighs, thinking about all this, and about the laundry and the cookies she has to make for her son's sleepover. Her lover will sleep until two and then get up and go out for coffee at a Starbucks where he makes calls on his cell to check on the arrangements he has made for the evening – which restaurants, which bars, which drugs, which girls. Jane would like to be going with him. But she needs to sleep, or she will have circles under her eyes. Her face will be puffy, her skin lusterless. She is older than the dancers her lover manages by ten years or more and she can't afford to let anything slip. She needs sleep but she can't sleep. She is with her lover, she is supposed to be happy, she will have circles under her eyes, she will be old, she will be ugly and

Jane is on the bus. The man sitting front of her is ugly. Not on the outside but in his heart, which she can see, and it is black. He is the devil, or perhaps a serial killer, and he is going to do something bad, which only Jane knows, since she can see his heart. The other people on the bus are eating their lunches, and pointing out of the windows at the sights. They are singing Beatles songs. The man turns to look at Jane and she realizes that he can see her heart, too. He knows that she knows. She has had this dream before, she remembers. Each time, she did not prevent the bad thing, which she can't remember, from happening. She resolves this time will be different. She fixes her mind on the man, on his hat, on the handkerchief he holds clutched in his hand, on the large red apple he is eating which his large white teeth.

It's his briefcase, she remembers. She has to steal his briefcase. When the other passengers break into "Rocky Raccoon," distracting him, she leaps up and grabs it and runs. The door bursts open and she jumps off the bus. This time, she thinks, sprinting through the park toward the river. This time, but he is gaining on her and the briefcase itself is growing larger. It drags from her hand, and she has to drop it and it bursts like a bomb

and Jane falls out of her dream, but not out of sleep. She sinks to a place where there are no dreams, although her face is still troubled, her lips drawn back a little, the corners of her eyes scrunched. She sleeps in this lower, dreamless darkness, while elements of the last dream detach themselves and rise, hanging in the air of the bedroom, the apple, the handkerchief, the briefcase. They join the other things that roost near the ceiling, -- the red buttons, the candlesticks, the answer cake, one of the floating house plants, the silver airplane, her mother's picture. They revolve like planets, slowly, slowly gathering around the bed, but Jane sleeps on, going deeper and deeper into the dark.

When she begins to rise again, it is almost dawn. The curtains are whitening in the new light. Each layer of sleep that Jane breaks through is sticky, like a burst soap bubble. She can feel the remnants clinging, trailing from her hair, her fingertips. Each layer is less dark, and that should be a good thing the coming of the light, but Jane is full of regret. Wait, she says, moving her lips soundlessly, let me try again, wait, but there is no more time, no more

no more, no more. Jane is awake. She has to go to the bathroom. She feels as if she hasn't slept at all. She is late, but she lies there, one arm across her eyes. She is so tired, so sad. She lies there with her eyes closed, trying not to think, feeling the heat from her lover's arm, his thigh. She lies there, not moving.

Something though is crouching in the corner. Some figure is sitting in the chair in the corner. Some dream creature. Something is opening the door to the bathroom, wanting a drink of water, or is creeping downstairs to look for something to eat, or to turn on the television. Something is opening the window to see what kind of day it is.

PMS: THE STORY

I'm trying to get the funding together again. It's a hot topic, for sure, but the funding types are all men, aren't they? White men, men in suits, light gray suits, can't stand the idea of a little blood in even the near vicinity of their herringbone, their summerweight wool. There are some women at the top, but they're the type who runs seventy-five miles a week so they don't have their periods anymore, haven't had a period in years, faint at the sight of a Stayfree Maxi, no use in asking them. So I'm working at the bar. Tips are good. It's a well-kept secret of filmmaking: barmaid, bartender. A few thousand good Saturday nights and you've got it made.

I've got a partner as well. It's not like this is some kind of crazy personal crusade – no there's me and there's Roma. Roma is the sensible type, I'm ideas. I'm fireworks, she's setting the fuses. I fizz, she stands by with the paper towels. We get together for lunch every week to brainstorm. Seriously. We huddle over our pb and j, our apples, our little boxes of raisins and we get down to business.

I want to make it clear, this is not all about me. This is not about my PMS or Roma's PMS. We have something much more universal in mind. Universal and intimate. Handheld cameras, natural lighting. A lot of exteriors. Women in the park, hunched on benches biting their fingernails with their kids playing heedlessly behind them on the monkey bars. Women watching TV commercials that are not supposed to make you cry but do. Women in cars pounding their heads on the steering wheel while the car radios are playing the song that they first heard in high school and they thought then that they were going to be a fucking Disney princess, and now at thirty-three, thirty-four, thirty-five, they know they're going to be working at Target selling discount face lotion and name brand strapless bras to some other broad before she goes off to the ball. Believe me, you'll love it.

PMS is the libretto of women's lives, that's our motto, mine and Roma's. Meaning, there's no point in saying word one about women when they're climbing the ovulation mountain, because they're not women then, they're egg cases, they're reproductive rockets, they're clinically insane. Just ask yourself: why else is she happy for no reason? Decks herself with bits of frippery to go to the grocery store? Sings when she scrubs out the toilet where for the five-hundredth time someone has splattered like he is the Jackson Pollock of pee? You don't know a woman who's off in that direction, you don't know her until she's coming down the other side, skiing out of control, the winds of change distorting her features, and she can see everything, in all directions, every bump, every sawed-off pine tree, every ravine and abyss. Just ask any man. Not that they are getting any input into the project.

But it's not going to be just tears and loathing and asking for a divorce and running to the bank to clean out the joint account on the way to the airport, oh, no. Way too depressing. Documentary does not have to equal depressing, as my film teacher said, God rest his dead soul. Mr. Deeter. Mr. Paul Deeter. He wasn't a big shot, and he hadn't made much money in films and, in fact, was making his living at his father's dry cleaning business which he took over when his father went out one day to buy a clothes brush and never came back. But he was all the teacher I ever wanted. A giant among teachers, a Mr. Chips of film classes. He ran these classes at the back of the dry-cleaning business, not for the money – how could he make any money to speak of from me and the ex-ballet dancer twins and the old Armenian from the senior center and Marie the ex-Marine? It was a labor of love. Documentary is not all boxcars and dirty miners' faces and starving children, Mr. Deeter said, although of course they have their place. But consider, he said, the roses, the sunshine, the bubbles rising in a glass of champagne. I can see him still, saying that, his middle finger pressed to his lips, his eyes raised to the ceiling, the chemical fumes from the dry cleaning seeping in under the door, and over all, the mechanical grinding of the clothes carousel. It was unforgettable, that's all I can say.

Damn it, I said to Roma, we'll find a way to get all that in, the roses, the bubbles. A balanced portrayal. You've got the weeping women, the raving women, the women facing the camera with a dead look in their eyes while they tell you how they had an impulse to take their fork at dinner and plunge it into their partner's wrist and watch blood spurt out of the four little holes. But also you have the happy moments, the triumphs: women eating chocolate, women who have found a doctor who would prescribe the good drugs, women who have gone out and bought shoes.

Also, we're thinking of a section on alternative treatments – Roma's idea. Sea salt, crystals, organic mud, acupuncture, the whole bit. Roma knows someone who is a PMS healer. This woman, Madame Phoom she calls herself, will only cure PMS. She says, according to Roma, that she was sent to this planet to be born into the earth body of a woman for the express purpose of healing all women out of slavery and pain and submission, and the way she's doing this is by curing PMS. According to her, PMS is what holds women back. It's like no matter what you've done during the month that was good and creative and achievement-oriented – started a novel, effectively sucked up to the boss, finally dealt with your relationship with your mother – at the end of the cycle, you can kiss all that goodbye, because for three to seven days, you rave and moan and undo half of what you've done. Two steps forward, three steps back. So Madame Phoom, for a fee which she figures on a sliding scale according to income (no one is turned away), will lay you down on her red velvet couch in this great Victorian room she has, all beads and fringe and glass-shaded lamps, and she will pass her hands over your spirit envelope, which is what she calls your body, and encourage the PMS critters (her own term) to pass out at the extremities.

Roma has had this done, and she said it was pleasant, very energizing. She said that afterward she felt as if she wanted to learn the Greek language, although before she was never good at languages, and had, in fact, gotten a C in Spanish. I want to emphasize that this has not made me a believer, but in keeping with another of Mr. Deeter's maxims, you've got to go where drama lives.

In my day to day life, I find very little support for my project. I'm not complaining. But sometimes it's hard to stand up under the onslaught of negativity. I never talk in the bar about anything that's important to me personally as I don't think it's professional, but in an unguarded moment, I once confided in the bar owner's unemployed son, Bick, who acts as an extra bouncer when necessary. Bick is a big lunk and always wears a cowboy hat, although this is not a country-western bar. He has his own stool at the bar with a little brass nametag he had made that says "Bick's Seat," and he lives in a trailer across the street from the bar, which is a convenience for his love life. The trailer is a complete mess, littered with months' worth of newspapers and empty glasses, and his refrigerator has only beer and chocolate pudding cups in it. Or so I hear. Anyway, I told him once about my film project, and how I was saving my tips, and my plans for life in general, which I won't go into here, and he listened with the appearance of interest, although I came to believe later that this was due to a couple of pills he had popped right before closing. And now, when he's in a mean mood, he brings it up at the bar. He sits there on his brass-labeled bar stool and has the nerve to make fun of me and my art and my contributions to possibly a better world. You wouldn't believe the guffaws, the snickers and snorts. These yahoos would be laughing out of the other side of their mouths if they were faced with a woman in full PMS with a blunt instrument. Let's see how funny it is then, Bick. About as funny as an ambulance, Bick, as funny as the emergency room. Even the women at the bar laugh at these cruel jokes, which I don't understand. Don't they know I'm doing it for them?

Most of the time I don't let it get to me though. I have a budget, I have a timeline. I've got subjects lined up, although it will be tricky, when we start filming, to adjust the shooting schedule to everyone's menstrual cycle. No good filming Mrs. Milly Furness or LaTanya Scardelli when they're high on ovulation, is it? Here is where Roma's talents come in. she's a whiz at spreadsheets, a genius. And she has set up a Facebook page to keep everyone informed as soon as shooting is a go, so that everyone involved is in contact with everyone else.

I don't know how this project could survive without Roma. It was she, for instance, who thought of having the subjects bring a totem object with them when they're filmed, something that represents for them the feelings and sensations of PMS. We've done some test sessions with this, and they were a wow. The women brought incredible things, very creative: balls of crumpled newspapers, handfuls of broken glass, photos of their mothers, baskets of hardboiled eggs, unsheathed knives. Some things were harder to explain, like the copy of Mao's little red book, or a jar full of pennies, but very interesting all the same. One woman brought a small tactical nuclear weapon, but we couldn't use it, you need a permit.

I'm trying to persuade Roma to be one of the subjects of the documentary herself. I want there to be a section entitled "PMS: Political Prisoners." This would focus on women who have lost their jobs or perhaps even their freedom because of actions taken when they were under the influence of the PMS hormone cocktail. Roma, for instance, used to have a high-paying job as the dean's secretary at a large university. The dean was an annoying if not evil man who often pushed his employees to the limits of their patience. They compensated for this by saying nasty things about him behind his back and stealing office supplies. All very healthy and American, really. Once after a particularly bad day, Roma, who was PMS+2 (which means she was two days into the PMS part of her cycle – unavoidably, we've developed some of our own jargon) joined a co-worker for coffee. Cathartically, they outlined a plan where all the people who annoyed them would be put on a plane which was set to blow up when it was over the ocean. The dean would be on this plane, where, as an extra touch, there would be no merlot (which he had a passion for) left in first class. Tears would come to your eyes if you could hear Roma explain the simple joy that this harmless fantasy gave her, the surge of fulfillment she felt when she determined that the dean would survive the first blast and be ejected from the plane at 35,000 feet, screaming all the way down.

Somehow this got back to the dean, and not only was Roma fired from her job, but he tried to prosecute her under the stalking laws. Of course, it was thrown out of court, but not until after Roma had considerable trouble and expense. Now, that story should be on film. But Roma sees herself as more of a behind-the-scenes person. She's not in it for the glory, she says, and I have to respect that, even though I've got the filmmaker's itch to get her on camera. As Mr. Deeter used to say, it's not real until it's on film.

As I say, I'm working on the funding. What we have now is a mixed bag. Every cent of my tips goes into the kitty. I'm living on my hourly wage which is tough but not impossible if I cut a few corners. I only drink at the bar where it's free, for instance. I cut coupons, go to bargain movies.

Living with Mom is a big help, although she's constantly threatening to throw me out, which causes a lot of stress. She wants me to get into a profession, go back to school, at least marry a guy who has a job. Whoever heard of a movie about PMS she says, it's disgusting, it's not nice. What you should make in a movie is something light, a comedy or a romance with some attractive outfits to look at. Fine, Mom, I say, why don't I just call up Ashton Kutcher and Jennifer Anniston and see if they're interested? Why don't I just make myself a Prozac, lettuce and tomato sandwich? Just because PMS is a thing of the past for you, screw it up for everyone else, why don't you? Really, she's mad because of the copper in the basement, something I bought for an investment when it looked like the price was going to go up in a big way. It's stacked in these neat rolls – fifty thousand feet of copper wire doesn't take up as much room as you'd think. But she complained that when she goes down to do the laundry she bumps into it and it cuts up her shins.

The copper is in the kitty. My little inheritance from Aunt Irene is in the kitty. My bingo wins – in the kitty – another sore point with Mom, since she claims she should have got a cut of the last one since she let me use her markers on the cover-up game. There's Roma's alimony – that's our operation money. I didn't want to take it, but she insisted. She says it's like money from a Mafia crime family, tainted with sin and bad vibes. Roma's ex-husband is a professor at a university (the same one where Roma worked for the dean), and according to Roma, uses his position to seduce young impressionable girls who are softened up by the poetry of Shelley and Keats. She says that she writes him a note once a month when she gets the check, informing him that, once again, she is donating it to the documentary and reminding him that his name will go in the credits.

I don't want you to think I'm obsessed. It's not like I don't have a life or any fun. I like fun as much as anybody. I like days at the beach, walks in the rain. I regularly play sand volleyball in good weather and I mall-walk when it's too cold. Roma and I get together every once in a while for a couple of glasses of wine and a good tearjerking movie. Mom and I take a t'ai chi class on Monday nights. Health is wealth, Mr. Deeter used to remind us, in our little after-class talks. Neglect the body, neglect the soul, and what is a documentary with no soul?

We used to go out sometimes to the bakery next to the dry cleaners after class and buy up a big bag of day-old doughnuts and sit on Mr. Deeter's back porch and just talk. Mr. Deeter would smile and nod and listen most of the time. We were all like kids to him, even old Mr. Arshtinian, who was seventy-eight. But sometimes we could persuade him to talk about his documentary-making past, and then everyone would shut up. I mean it, we were rapt.

Everything in his past life he remembered by what film he was making at the time. The '70s was industrial products and vacuum cleaners, plus a series of short subjects of people watching television. In the '80s he got fascinated by food and did a number of films on Jello, Cool Whip, mashed potatoes, instant pudding – he was very interested in a certain kind of texture at the time. He was sidetracked for a while by financial considerations: he did a few projects for a cosmetics company of women putting on makeup, but it was too restrictive. The company wanted all the women to look good, and were actually very angry when Mr. Deeter got some of the models to experiment with cross applications – you know, lipstick on their eyebrows, mascara instead of lipliner, and so on. But this led him to do some work with body painting – his film, *Red Breast, Blue Thigh*, won him a cult following. His interest in the human body continued in *Their Eyes Were Watching*, which is a beautifully choreographed, no-dialogue visual poem where the camera watches men watching women in old-fashioned underwear. In the '90s, he started his immense, seminal work on the relationship between Americans and their cars. When I view this stuff today I am in awe, I mean it. One of the best parts is where he snuck into people's back seats and filmed them driving until they noticed him and threw him out – really raw stuff, very powerful. That was when he got his hip injury, pushed out of a Volvo at forty-five mph.

Mr. Deeter: what an inspiration. I wish Roma could meet him, but unfortunately that's not going to happen. Mr. Deeter's wife cracked down on him and demanded that he cancel the classes. Wasn't it enough that he had sacrificed his art to the dry cleaning business? Apparently not. In my opinion, she couldn't stand it that he was having a little fun, and further, I believe that she thought Mr. Deeter and I were getting too close. She couldn't believe there wasn't a physical side to our relationship – the woman didn't understand the first thing about the community of art. She said she didn't like the idea of her husband discussing intimate physical details with another woman, which is just another example of how PMS is marginalized in our society. And, of course, now he's dead.

Whenever I have a particularly brilliant idea, I think about Mr. Deeter. He's in my mind when Roman and I are looking at footage in her rumpus room, which we try to do once a month, a regular date. She makes popcorn and chocolate chip cookies and I buy the root beer. Sometimes I have to bring Mom, if she's having one of her bad days and can't be left alone in the house – which is a drag because she continually makes comments and, worse, noises, to let us know her opinion. (She's a champion snorter, I'll give her that.)

And I think of Mr. Deeter when I persuade a subject to go a little farther than she meant to. Like when LaTanya, who is in her fifties, told how her mother never said a thing to her about getting her period and she had to piece it together from reading the *Reader's Digest* ("I am Josephine's Uterus") and from anatomical drawings on the sidewalk in colored chalk – I swear I felt Mr. Deeter's hand on my shoulder while I was filming. Roma independently said she felt a presence in LaTanya's kitchen with its apple-shaped potholders and alphabet refrigerator magnets that her husband had arranged to spell out "BUY BEER." Roma says she felt something that would look like a mist if she could have seen it, possibly rainbow-colored and with an accompanying odor of cilantro. This really blew me away, because Mr. Deeter loved Thai food – I'm not kidding.

LaTanya was oblivious to all this, but she had her mind on other things. She had never told anyone this stuff before and she couldn't believe she was doing it then, in front of the camera, when she was supposed to be making Chicken Marengo in time for when her husband was bringing his mother over for dinner, a weekly event. Her mother-in-law hates LaTanya because she's black, and LaTanya is trying to get in her good graces. She really freaked when she realized she'd spent most of her dinner preparation time in front of the camera. Roma and I pitched in though. Roma loves to cook and she really threw herself into that Chicken Marengo.

I set the table and lit the candles, all the time thinking about Mr. Deeter and how he would have loved LaTanya. The man didn't have a prejudiced bone in his body. Skin tones were what he was interested in – how they took the light, how they reproduced on film. The man was a genius with skin – it was a landscape to him, a geography. He was a geologist of the skin. There's always something under there, he'd say, and it's the duty of the documentarian to show it. "You've got to get under it, but you've got to stay on top of it." What an epigrammist. I've got that one on the wall over my desk, in calligraphy, a gift from Roma. She gave it to me for the six-month anniversary of our working together and I'm not ashamed to admit I had tears in my eyes when I thumbtacked it to the wall.

When I met Roma, I was at a low point. I couldn't see a way to go on without Mr. Deeter. This was not long after his funeral. I couldn't stand being home with Mom. She was trying to be supportive, but her idea of supportive was that I should join her women's church group, of which she is entertainment chairman. She arranges one-day trips to local sights with a spiritual component, like the house of the guy who has made a model of the Vatican out of bottle caps.

I took extra shifts at work. I rode the buses, all night sometimes. I'd walk past Mr. Deeter's dry cleaning business, my footsteps slowing as I looked in the window, trying to convince myself that he wasn't really gone. I had to wear a disguise when I did this because his wife (who I won't dignify with the title of Mrs. Deeter) was on the lookout for me. If she recognized me, she'd come out and yell abusive things and some-times throw hangers. I even went and visited the others, the old group – the twins, and old Mr. Arshtinian, and Marie, the vet. But it was no good – our mortar was gone and we were like crumbling bricks scattered on a weed-strewn ground.

It was a bad time. I did some things I'm ashamed of. For in-stance, I slept with Bick. Right, you're appalled, I understand. How could I sleep with a fake cowboy, a yahoo who makes fun of serious subjects, who spent fifty dollars on a customized name plate for where he parks his butt? Well, this one Tuesday, three weeks after Mr. Deeter's funeral, it was a glacially slow night at the bar. I was closing by myself, no one in the place except for some drunks stumbling around on the dance floor. Bick showed up half an hour before closing and bought me a drink. Pointless, since I can have a drink an hour as officially stipulated in my contract, but it was a nice gesture, or so I thought at the time. "You look blue," he said to me. "You look like you need some cheering up."

I'm sure I did. But did I need to go over to Bick's trash-littered trailer and spend the night on his stale sheets, probably the same sheets from the last woman he'd bought with a pre-mixed daiquiri? I knew it was more or less a rebound thing even when he was whomping away on top of me and I was hanging on to his neck for dear life, trying to keep out of the way of his hat brim. He likes to wear his cowboy hat in bed, no clothes, just the hat. (It was a rebound thing in a symbolic way. I mean, I want to make it clear that my relationship with Mr. Deter was strictly platonic – he was a mentor, I was a mentee – no matter what his wife thinks.)

But anyway, you can see how low I'd sunk, eating chocolate pudding for breakfast from Bick's refrigerator, telling him my secret dreams and plans while he tried to kill a fly by snapping at it with his belt. What would have happened if I hadn't met Roma, I don't know. I might be married to Bick right now, knocked up with a little Bick or Bickette, relining his bureau drawers with flowered Contac paper, trying to get the mysterious yellow-green stain off his refrigerator shelves. I might think I was happy, I might be thinking of sex with Bick as my reason for living, and looking back on my documentary-making days as the kind of past that you make fun of after a few drinks.

But – I did meet Roma. I had gone to the supermarket to pick up some chocolate pudding to take over to Bick's. He likes Swiss Miss, and I found myself incredibly angry about that. You know that PMS anger, how it comes over you in a big wave, how you feel crushed by it but also like you're riding it, anger bolts shooting out of your fingertips? That was how I felt when I stood there holding a six-pack of Swiss Miss Milk Chocolate. I hate Swiss Miss, it's insipid. Hershey's is the only way to go in chocolate pudding, but Bick would not have it in the trailer. I was hormonal, I was bloated, I was practically hallucinating, and he wanted the bland, watered-down chocolate of Swiss Miss, chauvinistically named and decorated with the picture of a repressed maiden in anachronistic and uncomfortable clothing. I gritted my teeth and closed my eyes and let the wave wash over me. When I opened my eyes, there was chocolate pudding sprayed all over the place, squeezed violently out by my clenched fist. The dairy case manager threatened me with his floor mop and who knows what might have happened if not for Roma.

She stepped right up to him, an imposing woman in yoga pants and wearing a bicycle helmet. "Can't you see that this woman is having a PMS emergency?" she said to him. She got right in his face, I can tell you. Later, over mochaccinos and chocolate croissants, we couldn't help but laugh at the look he had on him. Nothing could have brought us together faster, not to mention that it showed us how we might have a dream in common. She came home with me that night, because we couldn't stop talking and making lists. I called Bick and told him what he could do with his Swiss Miss. Roma and I were exploding with ideas. She slept on the couch and stayed over for breakfast although Mom refused to cook anything except oatmeal without raisins.

We've been together ever since, overcoming every difficulty, facing every challenge. We admire each other, support each other. Some might say that because Roma is not a documentarian, per se, that she is the lightweight of the partnership. But although Roma does not consider herself an artist (or "artiste," as she likes to say), to me she is the essence of creativity, a woman who has taken up the poor threads of her life and woven them into a garment of beauty and excellent fit. Mom is totally wrong when she calls Roma a man-hater and a dried-up old cranberry.

But, you may say, what's the point of all this creativity, this energetic partnership, this marshalling of resources, this focusing of our daily lives and thoughts? Who cares if there's a documentary about PMS, or another documentary at all? When the documentary category comes on at the Academy Awards, doesn't everybody go to the bathroom or make themselves a cheese and peanut butter sandwich?

All I can say is what Mr. Deeter said before me. Documentary is life, life is documentary. Get up in the morning, brush your teeth, spit, change your socks: if I have a camera on you, that's documentary. If I put it in front of an audience, it's a hymn to the universality of the human experience. And for the documentary maker, there's an unexpected benefit. When you have a camera in your hand, you always have a reason to be there, wherever there is. You never in your life have to feel de trop, out of place, a third wheel, last one picked for the team. You're there. You're the camerawoman. You're on the trail of documentary.

Just one more word about the whole Mr. Deeter thing. It's true that we did have some tender passages. But there was nothing that, if anyone had been filming it, wouldn't have been PG. Not so much as a kiss. Yes, we held hands in the back room of the dry cleaners, after the other students had left. Yes, we discussed, perhaps fervently, how our lives might have been different if we'd met in some other place, some other time. There was some silly but oh-so-sweet talk about reincarnation, how we might have been lovers in nineteenth-century Paris or the steppes of Russia. Mr. Deeter might have allowed that Mrs. Deeter wasn't perfectly in tune with his dreams or the physical side of his nature, and certainly, I complained bitterly about Mom. But it was innocent. There wasn't any question of sex or divorce, not, I'll admit, because of my morality and restraint. I was heated up and ready for the Motel 6. But Mr. Deeter was a gentleman, a saint. We can't do it, he said, and I had to respect that if it killed me.

So, yeah, maybe I had some guilt when Mrs. Deeter threw the hangers. I sinned in thought, if not in deed, as the priests used to say. A good thing, in a way, that it was Mr. Deeter that died, in the sense that if it was me, I'd be somewhere a lot hotter, and he, dear sweet man, is surely plucking a harp, thinking of what kind of light in which to film the angels. The good die young they say. (Not that he was all that young – he was a good deal older than me, but very vital.) The wicked are left on this earth to mourn and do what they can. That's where I take my comfort: I have a plan, a mission, a continuation of Mr. Deeter's life and work where he would have wanted it – on film.

Meanwhile, Roma and I are in the documentary trenches. We've scraped the money together for several hours of filming (Roma has taken a second job – she's doing the newsletter for SPASOV, the Society for the Preservation and Spread of Voodoo; and I've applied for a grant for indigent filmmakers from a foundation headed by Johnny Depp. Mrs. Furness has agreed to be treated by Madame Phoom. Mrs. Furness, Milly, has a highly cinematic form of PMS – it makes her scream. She has to scream, or she believes the veins in her head will explode and she will have a stroke. This has caused her untold anguish and brought societal wrath down on her. She is banned from every mall in town and most restaurants. If she wants to go out to eat, the only place she can go is to the TickTock Diner on Olde Route 36 where the counterman is totally deaf.

We're planning to follow her around town while she screams and gets thrown out of places. She has agreed to wear an outfit in jarring colors – orange and chartreuse is what we settled on – to show visually her inner conflict and rage. Then I'm thinking a shot outside where she just screams at the sky for a whole minute. Maybe two. I'm hoping for clouds, looming cumulo-nimbus boiling and shifting behind her head. Close-ups of her mouth – we'll take the camera practically down her throat, as if we could see her inner hormonal torment. And then off to Madame Phoom's – the couch, the soothing music, the graceful hands of Madame weaving a pattern over Milly's prostrate body. Madame Phoom is going to have her nails done at her cousin's nail boutique with gold sparkles and with the right lighting and camera speed they'll leave little trails of light behind them.

Madame Phoom's treatment, even at the discount Roma negotiated, is not cheap, and she's making us pay for the nail job, but I think it will be worth it. Mr. Deeter would say, go for it. Love documentary, he would say, hold it dear. Put it before your wife, your child, your breakfast cereal, your morning cigarette – and so we will. Whatever happens, we'll be there. If Milly Furness rises from the red velvet couch and stands cured, composed and unscreaming, the camera will be rolling. If the PMS critters come flying out from her body as Madame Phoom claims they will, the camera will be rolling. And even if nothing at all happens and there is just the red velvet of the couch and Madame Phoom's disappointed face and Milly still screaming her head off, mouth open, teeth glistening with saliva, the camera will damn well still be rolling, and that's the point.

MY SISTER'S HAIR

At the Opera

    I was listening to a soprano hacking away at Carmen, trying to distract myself from her phrasing by looking at the people around me. I was first introduced to opera by a four-record set of Maria Callas singing Carmen, and it has made me a very severe fan. Anything, anything to take my mind off this woman's panting, I mean it – panting, like a dog trying to sing a scale. There was plenty to look at, thank heaven, but I like to be selective, I like to catalog if I can and so I was looking at hair. I was counting the various colors in the rows in front of me (only four, I had a marvelous seat). Three red, twelve brown, sixteen blonde – probably only three of which were natural, twenty-three gray or white. The opera audience is an older one. There were a few heads out of my line of sight and I waited patiently for the ranks of the listeners to shift so that I could see them, pinching the flesh on the inside of my wrist to keep my mind off the soprano. A very demure chignon, gray. Another brunette, curled and sprayed to a turn. And then, such a shock, I put my hand to my throat, an instinctive, useless gesture – although what instinct does it serve? The man next to me murmured sympathetically, thinking I had been moved by the soprano's buzz-saw vibrato, but I ignored him. It was my sister's hair, in the front row – long, shining, straight, neither blonde nor brunette – although I very quickly, in one second or less, saw that it was not my sister, nor exactly her hair. It was maybe the tiniest bit more blonde, with a spring at the crown hers didn't have, but almost identical to her old hair, her hair of thirty and more years ago. I sat back in my seat, sighing. "Yes, isn't it wonderful?" the man next to me said, trying to take one of my hands. What a pervert. I wished I had a hat pin to stab him with but no one wears those anymore. I had only my steely eye with which to pierce him. Silly, I thought, placing my purse as a barrier between us. To be so moved by the sight of my sister's hair, my sister's almost hair, as if we were estranged or she were dead or in another country, when she lives only on the east side in a condominium with a pool and a sauna and a whirlpool. Ridiculous, I said to myself, removing my foot from the sly touch of the sex maniac next to me. But still, I gazed at it with fondness, more fondness than I have ever felt for my own hair.

Color

My hair used to be brown actually, it still is sometimes brown. Once you start dyeing your hair, there's no reason to stick to a color is there? You've already introduced the concept of fake so I've had brown, blonde, black. Not red – my husband didn't like red, it was a concession. What can I say? I haven't always been the woman I hoped to be. Black only for a little while – it made me look sinister, too pale and vampire-like. But the thing is that through all the colors, I looked more or less the same to myself. Spiritually, I had brown hair, no matter what. And spiritually, my sister has blonde. When she was a child, angelic blonde. Later, darker blonde. Someone unkind might have called it dishwater. But I am not unkind, or not in this instance, for whatever color you wanted to call it, my sister's former hair was beautiful. We have pictures taken when each of us was three, in the same sailor suit which my mother saved for this purpose, our curls arranged in more or less the same artless way. I look perky, possibly mischievous, an undertone of dissatisfaction. She looks angelic, charmed, ready for a blessed and magical existence.

The Braid

I walked away from the opera in a pensive mood, dodging up and down the aisles and ducking into the ladies' room, to shake off the demented man in the next seat. He asked me for my phone number, can you imagine? "Please," I said, "we're both overseventy. Get some counseling." Walking down the street, looking for a cab although I didn't really expect to find one at that hour, I debated whether I still had the braid of my sister's hair that had been cut off when she was twelve. I had had it for a long time, but who knows where it is now. It's not so easy to explain why I kept it. I didn't keep the length of my own hair that was cut off at about the same age. I watched the chunks and clumps of my own hair fall to the floor of the hairdresser's cubicle with complete indifference. I was expecting to be changed into a teenager and was anxious for this transformation to be complete. The hairdresser was my mother's. She was named Tawney. It was never clear to me whether this was her first or last name. She was short and cushiony, European-looking, soft and aunt-like, with a gamin hairstyle, lots of pointed wisps of hair stabbing her cheeks. She cut my hair into a style that she said was called "Marienbad." I imagined it had something to do with Maid Marian, who I had wanted to be when I read about Robin Hood. While my mother counted out the tip, Tawney swept my hair into a dustpan and dropped it into a pink plastic wastebasket. My sister, though, had her hair cut off at home, I don't know why – an economy measure? Tawney terminally booked up? My mother cut her hair off while it was braided, so it fell to the floor all together. I gathered it up and tied it with a blue grosgrain ribbon, while my mother competently shaped the ends. It pains me that I don't remember what I was thinking. It might have been a result of reading books of the last century, where the characters were always preserving mementos, tied with ribbons, immured in enamel boxes or old trunks in the attic. Maybe I was playing out a part, one of the girls in *Little Women*. My sister didn't care that I had taken her hair, or didn't notice. She didn't want it for herself.

Inheritance

None of our children has inherited the color of my sister's hair. They are all brunettes. Red hair is said to run in my mother's family, but none of us has got it. Both of my daughters inherited a cowlick just to the left of the crowns of their heads from their father, which made it impossible to cut their hair attractively when they were children. My sister, cowlickless, for many years cut her own hair, standing in front of the mirror and pulling it forward over her face so she could see what she was doing. I never had the nerve to do this, although I did have the nerve once to let the husband of one of my friends cut my hair when he was stoned out of his mind on hash.

The Marines

After the opera, I sat drinking chocolate-covered-cherry decaf, thinking, in a little coffee place, trying to warm my feet. My circulation has never been the same since I quit smoking. All the health benefits I believed I would enjoy failed to materialize. My allergies are definitely worse, for instance. As I've said, my sister's hair darkened as she grew older. No longer the angelic blonde, when she was seventeen, her hair was an ethereal color not quite ash blonde. I was married by then, too early, according to my mother – don't you hate it when they're right? I was living in another state, on or near a Marine base. My sister and I hadn't seen each other for more than a year and she was coming out to visit. I was not much of a housekeeper then, and my only preparation for her arrival was to find some sheets for the couch and buy a few bottles of Boone's Farm Apple Wine. I had, not only a husband, but a baby, and we lived more or less happily as the married-couple center of a group of Marines who were glad to have somewhere to go that was off the base. Anybody's sisters were of great interest to these Marines. We had a picture of mine from the summer before when she was on vacation with my parents. She was sitting on a rock in a beach area, back arched, legs hooked to one side, very pin-up. She was wearing a colorful little knitted hat and out from under it streamed the lengths and tresses of her hair. After a flirtation with very short hair in junior high, she had, as all the girls were doing then, grown it out. She had the hair of the time – the seventies – very long, past her shoulder blades, shiny and very straight. She didn't need, as some did, to iron it. Even without the hair, she looked good, but it was her hair in this picture, sent out of state to our off-base home, which seduced a score of Marines – lusting, drooling in advance over the honey-colored lengths of her hair. Any of them would have volunteered to climb up that hair, would have braved a witch, gathered rampion. I left the picture out, casually, on the kitchen counter, next to the toaster. If I had had a better furnished household, I could have displayed it on the coffee table, but it was a rental place, we had nothing of our own except a stereo, three boxes of albums, a crib, and a playpen. The Marines would pick her photo up when they were getting a beer, or a glass of Boone's Farm. What a honey, what a babe, they would say, but respectfully, since she was my sister. She looked, they said, cool, righteous, groovy. I would recite the facts: her name, her age, that her eyes were blue, that she was blonde. I would say these things jogging the baby on my hip, trying to get her to drink some apple juice.

The Marines offered various enticements: they would take her horseback riding, to swim in the reservoir, out to the desert to see the stars, for a ride on their motorcycles. There was not much to do in that town, after all, except make the rounds of the bars. When she came, she favored the least rambunctious among them, a Christian Scientist who took her to an amusement park with his mother and sister, while all the James Dean look-alikes, the dark brooding soulful poets on motorcycles postured in vain. She was not a girl who liked her men to be difficult. She and the Christian Scientist Marine often took the baby with them as a chaperone, and fed her things she wasn't supposed to have – chocolate ice cream for instance, which gave her diarrhea. During my sister's visit, it snowed for the first time in years, and everywhere the desert was dusted over with white.

Dyeing

I began to dye before my sister, naturally, since I am older. We both found our first gray hairs in our twenties. I was sitting on the patio at our parents' house and my mother said, "you're starting to go gray, aren't you." I was twenty-six, young enough to think that this was funny. At first, I only got my hair streaked. A sort of shower cap was placed on my head and strands of hair tweaked out through tiny holes by a wicked instrument that looked like a crochet hook. It created a sort of optical illusion that does not cover the gray, but distracts from it. Later, I went the rest of the way – serious, all-over color, which is applied with a small paintbrush. My sister's hair, being lighter than mine, took longer to show the gray. She has always dyed it the same color, a sort of constancy I admire but cannot emulate. She dyes it blonde, the blonde of her youth, the angelic blonde. We share a hairdresser, quite unlike the enigmatic Tawney. Ours is called Gina, very slender, with waist-length hair. She does our heads in her basement, and has a small son who sometimes tries to shut the door in the face of the customers. "Go away," he will say, and I have to wait until Gina comes to open the door and shoo him away to play with his trucks.

Twins

If my sister had been at the coffee shop with me, drinking café mocha, which is what she likes, the waitress would very likely ask if we were twins. People do this more and more, as if we were growing to look more alike as we get older, even if my hair is a quite dark brown with red highlights, as it is now, and hers is the angelic blonde. We say we don't mind this, but perhaps we are getting a tiny bit bored? "No," we say. "We're sisters." Everyone smiles. As it was, the waitress said nothing. There was hardly anyone in the coffee shop that late at night, and no one in it looked like anyone else. I sipped my cooling decaf and looked out the window. In it, I could see myself reflected, sipping, and also, vaguely, the dark forms and movement s of the street outside. People were passing, hurrying, for it was cold. Occasionally, someone would open the door and come in. Sometimes someone outside came up close to the window and, cupping his hands, looked inside.

Scarlet Fever

Both my sister and I had scarlet fever. I was enchanted to have it, since it seemed such an old-fashioned, even a literary disease. Children in books had scarlet fever. Didn't Caddie Woodlawn, or one of the Five Little Peppers have scarlet fever? I had a mild case. They still used to quarantine you with scarlet fever then, so I stayed home from school first for myself and then for my sister, a total of six weeks in all. We both got our hair cut off, for confused and contradictory reasons. One of my aunts said it was because the hair drew strength from the body, but it seems more likely that our mother didn't want to have to comb our pillow-tossed locks every day and make us cry. Even short, our hair got very tangled. My sister's hair would be standing up all over her head when she was delirious, talking and crying in a cracked voice. She had a much worse case than I did. She was known as the sickly sister. Later she got burrs in her hair and my mother thought it would have to be cut off again, but our aunt applied an old folk remedy, vinegar, and sat patiently combing out each aid-darkened lock. She smelled of pickles for a while after that, no matter how often my mother washed her hair.

Dating

Another thing my sister would do if she were at the coffee shop: look around for possible men. My sister is always trying to get me to come over to her condominium and mingle. She wants me to swim in the pool and sweat in the whirlpool or the sauna, then go to the juice bar with her and sit around drinking mango smoothies. All this to meet men. If she had been at the opera, she would have advised me to get to know the pervert better. Or rather, she would have encouraged me with looks and nudges. Times have changed since I shopped her picture around to Marines. As she was not sitting with me in the coffee shop, however, I turned my chair so that I was facing away from the other customers. When we were young, our dating years only slightly overlapped. Once I took my sister to a mixer, to give her a preview of high school. (I still hate the work, "mixer," which brings to mind the whirling, mangling electric beaters of the kitchen appliance.) I introduced her to a boy on whom she used to have a crush, but she had forgotten who he was, or anyway didn't recognize him. After that, I was distracted because the boy I had broken up with four months before was there, and consequent on the playing of what had been our song, "Hang On, Sloopy," by the McCoys, we got back together and spent some time making out in the janitor's closet. Later, when I had already started going out with the man I married, I fixed my sister up with a friend of his to out to a bar where Leon Redbone was playing, when he still played music that was not for commercials and sitcom theme songs. The friend was someone my future husband worked with at the library, and who was known, I hope not unkindly, as The Dummy, because he seldom spoke. He had remarked on more than one occasion, in thrifty sentences, how much he liked my sister's hair.

Permanence

My sister's hair is no longer straight, by the way. She has been getting a permanent for some time, from Gina, our beloved hairdresser. I was the first to find Gina, when she still worked at Hair Wizard. I went there originally because it was only a block from where I worked. When Gina left to have her own business, my sister and I followed her. Our mother hates my sister's permanent, and never lets a chance pass to tell her so. I like it, and even wish sometimes to have one of my own, but Gina won't let me. I understand that my sister wants her hair to have a bit of life, not just to lie there. It's true that she had to wash it every day when she was young or it would look lank and limp. Once she gave this as an excuse to a boy who asked her out – she said that she had to wash her hair. She was upset when I told her that this was what you told boys when you were giving them the brush-off. She had meant it: she did have to wash her hair. She was and is a truthful person, always, unlike me. I am not a liar, but I like to embellish the story. In the coffee shop, when

I went up to get a refill, the waitress asked me what I was reading. I said *Anna Karenina.* She asked if I liked it. I said, "yes." Now if I were telling this story, I might say we discussed how I read Anna Karenina three times when I was trying to get a divorce. I was not interested in throwing myself from a train, only in having a lover like Vronsky. The waitress might have been getting a divorce – she looked dissatisfied. We might have exchanged emails and met for lunch later on. I might have become a significant influence in her life, perhaps later on introducing her to the man whom she would marry more happily. I was not the person who introduced my sister to her husband. She met him in a bar when I was out of state with the Marine.

Weddings

At the second refill, I learned that the waitress was indeed married, not from conversation, but from the ring on her finger. Her hair though did not look to me like a married woman's hair – too hopeful, I would call it, too much time had gone into it – but perhaps she hadn't been married long. Both my sister and I got married in June, but years apart. I married, as pointed out by my prescient mother, too young. My sister waited until a more seemly age: twenty-four. For my wedding, which took place in 1969, we both got our hair done by Tawney. Tawney incorporated into my hair a matching hairpiece which gave me a sort of Victorian nest of curls on which my white cloud of wedding veil perched. My sister's hair was more an evocation of the early sixties – a smooth French twist with the top hair elaborately ratted and looped. She looked like the love interest in a James Bond movie, one of the ones with Sean Connery. Our hair was done the day before, so we had to maintain the integrity of the "do" for almost eighteen hours. We slept uneasily and then got up to stand outside on the patio and smoke in the dawn light. At my sister's wedding in 1976 our hair was more relaxed. We did not have it done. My sister's hair was in its glory, long and the color of wheat when a cloud has passed over the sun.

Pain

In the cab, which I miraculously caught as I waited for a light to change, I snagged my nail on the torn fabric of the seat. There was no use in complaining to the cab driver, but I did anyway. I explained to him how easy it would be to sew a patch over the gaping expanse of cheap padding material from which a quite sharp spring protruded. Or even attach one with tape, duct tape is the kind I would recommend, cheap and easy to use. He said, "do I got time to do that?" It isn't that I can't take pain. I have a relatively high pain tolerance, but this doesn't mean that I like it.

Performance

In the cab I thought what I might do when I got back to my apartment. I hate to be unoccupied. I can't even watch television without doing something else at the same time, clipping coupons, for instance, or bookmarking recipes on Pinterest. I thought I might listen to the Maria Callas Carmen record and flagellate myself for not having been born early enough to have heard her live. Of course, technically, I was born early enough, but I didn't form my passion for opera until well after Callas's prime. Calling it a passion is probably misleading. I'm not an expert or a maven. I like to go once or twice a year. I dislike light opera and anything sung in English. Our parents used to take my sister and me to the theater, for our cultural good. We saw a number of plays and musicals. We were always putting on our good dresses and going out at night, our long hair streaming down our backs. My sister had one going-to-the-theater dress that was blue. When she wore it, with a matching ribbon in her hair, someone invariably came up and compared her to Alice in Wonderland. I felt at the time that my own outfit was far superior – a pink, princess-waisted dress with a matching sweater. However, it attracted no one's notice.

Dying

Our aunt told us many times how she planned to have her hair done by her hairdresser for her appearance at her own funeral. She was adamant that she didn't want the hairdresser employed by the mortician to do her hair. She felt that no one but Bobbie understood how to make her hair look its fullest and smoothest. She was worried that Bobbie, who was about her own age, would die before her. She urged Bobbie to lose weight and watch her cholesterol, bringing her healthful, low-fat snacks when she went for her weekly appointment. Our aunt had also planned what dress to wear. Everyone in the family knew – she didn't trust her husband to remember, even though she had it set aside in a carefully-labeled garment bag. White, she said, was flattering if worn next to the face. My sister is not worried about the hair of her corpse. She plans to be cremated, although her children don't like the idea. I haven't decided. I like the idea of being frozen and possibly defrosting in a world where a cure has been found for everything, but my sister refuses to consider it.

Trees

At the door of my apartment building, I stopped for a minute to look at the outlines of the tree branches against the night sky, even though the doorman was peering out at me and shaking his head. The trees outside of my apartment are not very satisfactory, skinny and with only a few leaves even in the height of summer. It's not that I grew up in the country, but we did have a yard with a maple tree, two mulberry trees, a blue spruce, and a spreading yew. Only one of the mulberries was climbable. My sister once caught her hair on a branch high up, almost level with the upstairs bedroom windows. A loop of her pony-tailed hair got hooked on a tiny curving spike and she couldn't see well enough to get free. I climbed up from below and unhooked her. The leaves of the tiny branch stayed in her hair for the rest of the afternoon. Nowadays I don't even like to look over the rail of an escalator, but at the age of ten or eleven I performed such feats casually, ignoring the fact that I was twenty feet off the ground. My sister and I once climbed onto the garage roof from the mulberry tree, but when we got there, we found that there was nothing to do. As I turned my face to the sky, the doorman turned away, pretending to ignore me. He complains that going up and down in the elevator aggravated his sinus condition, also, opening and closing the door makes his bursitis worse. He doesn't like visitors, believing that they carry unfamiliar and therefore more potent germs. Really, he wishes we would all stay in our apartments all day and all night.

Next Door

My next-door neighbors are a married couple. The wife has a job she goes to and the husband works at home on the computer. He spends a great deal of time hanging around in the hall or the basement laundry room. Their apartment is full of waving green leaves and aquariums. It's as hot and humid as a jungle. He refers to all the plants by their Latin names, which I can't stand. When I come home in the daytime, I use the stairs because he listens for the sound of the elevator and ambushes anyone who gets off. But at night it's safe, he's got his wife in there to bore and annoy. The elevator moved up in silence, since the doorman was angry with me for standing so long outside looking at the branches of the trees and the sky. I knew that he had been waiting for me to come in so he could go to the bathroom. I could tell by the way he was standing but too bad. Why should I cut short my contemplation of nature? Why didn't he go on his break? I was planning to call my sister and tell her about the woman in the front row with her hair, almost her hair. I was planning to describe it minutely, the exact shade it was, how far off her own, the hair ornament the woman was wearing which was quite lovely, amber-colored glass and leather, something my sister herself might very well have chosen. I was planning to say how I hadn't seen the woman's face, and also how bad the soprano had been. I planned not to mention the sex maniac.

Fighting

I sat on my couch, which had had cleaned only the week before, sipping a glass of wine. I had gotten out the Maria Callas records. They came as a boxed set, a red box, very attractive. On the front there was a picture of Maria Callas herself. Her hair in the picture was very dark, black and lustrous. Our mother, as I said, believed in exposing us to culture, and these records were a part of that program. We had only a few records, maybe twenty, and they were an odd assortment. There was a record of someone reading from the book, *Heidi*, I remember, and an album of "Music for Dining" with a picture on the front of a couple in evening dress looking at each other intently in the light of some long candles. We had also a record of DeeDee Sharp singing "Mashed Potatoes," although this was not part of the culture program. My sister and I used to lie on the dining room floor and listen to these records and others. We used to lie under the old play table where, when we were younger, we had crayoned and pasted things. My sister's hair would be spread carelessly over the dining room rug, tangled sometimes around the legs of the play table. Sometimes we would fight over which record to play next. We were very physical fighters. I had the advantage, of course, since I was three years older, and bigger. Also meaner, I regret to say. I once gave my sister a black eye, although it was by accident. That is, I meant to hit her, but I forgot I was wearing my high school ring. But when we were younger, lying under the play table, it was mostly slapping and hair-pulling. My sister's hair was longer than mine then and more accessible. I can remember very well what it felt like in my fingers thick, silky and alive, the separateness of the strands sliding over each other. It was still the angelic color then, but beginning to darken. When I pulled my sister's hair, I could feel how it gave only to a certain point, which, when I tried it on myself I could see was the result of how the scalp pulled away from the bone of the skull and then held. Sitting on my couch, I put the wine glass down and pulled my hair experimentally – the sensation of give was still the same, although my hair is so much shorter and dryer and older.

Moving

When we were younger, my sister and I planned to live together when we were old. Our family has a history of long life, and we figured we were likely to outlive our husbands. We planned to live in an old house and always to wear blue jeans and tennis shoes, to keep cats and be eccentric. When we discovered we were allergic to cats, and indeed, to all fur-bearing animals, we said we would keep lizards. This was a plan we would tell to people at parties and everybody would laugh. We thought our husbands didn't mind, but perhaps they did. Now, we live, as I said, across town from each other, she in her condominium and I in my apartment. We are not estranged. But we have made no move toward the blue-jean-wearing, lizard-keeping existence. Perhaps we are not old enough yet. We go shopping together for clothes. We rarely buy anything, but we like to talk in the dressing rooms while we try things on. We go out for coffee (one café mocha, one decaf), and sometimes to the movies. My sister doesn't like opera. We go to poetry readings at book-stores and coffee houses and write notes that we slide back and forth to one another under cover of the coffee cups and crumbed plates.

My Sister's Hair

When I was waiting for the elevator under the cold eyes of the doorman, I supposed I might look for the braid of my sister's hair once I got into the apartment, just to check the color. How close was it to the hair of the woman in the front row? But once inside, this struck me as unproductive and melancholy. Also, although the end of the braid is lovely and wispy and pointed in the comma shape that braided hair makes, the other end, where it was cut from her head, is ragged and torn-looking. It looks violent, unnatural. I blame my mother, really. She should have cut it unbraided (although it would have been harder to keep that way), or she should have taken her to Tawney, no matter the cost. Sometimes, now, my sister and I go to Gina together, and she does us both at once. It's a convenience for Gina, since there is a good deal of waiting around for both my sister's permanent and my all-over dye job. Gina can overlap these tasks and make twice as much money for the hour and a half, which she needs, since she is more or less the sole support of her little boy. Gina has only one beauty shop chair in her basement, so the one of us who is not being worked on sits on a regular kitchen chair leafing through magazines. The last time we were there, I sat, looking at *Cosmopolitan*, which I never read at any other place, watching Gina's quick fingers move in my sister's hair, both in reality and in the mirror. Gina's ipod was playing a bouncy theme song from an old television show about six friends, three male and three female, who sleep with each other off and on. Gina, although she is half Italian, does not like opera, and doesn't care much about Maria Callas. "You know," my sister said to me, "we're not getting any younger." I didn't reply since I hate it when she says this, and also had come to a place in *Cosmo* where it promised to tell me the sexual secrets of successful businesswomen, not that I will ever need them. "You're lucky to have each other," Gina said, her hands smoothing and snipping and ruffling the permanented strands of the angelic-colored hair, but I didn't reply. The snippets of my sister's hair were falling to the floor and glittering there like stars.

UP LATE

The candle is going out, Jean said. Put your hand around it, please. Jean was always very polite. I always loved it how polite she was. I had known her for a long time. Two years and three months. Maybe that doesn't seem long. We were fourteen.

We lay close together under the porch. This was the kind of porch that has a lot of space underneath, with crosswise slats on the sides or some kind of thing that lets light in. You find wood under porches sometimes, or chunks of concrete or old furniture. Rolls of snow fence. Clay flowerpots stacked up or knocked over so that all or some of them are broken. Under this porch it was empty, just dirt and cold leaves that had blown in.

It was nothing for us to be lying close together. We had had sex already, and even slept together in a bed, Jean's bed, for almost one whole night. There, under the porch, we lay together for warmth, and for the excitement. We could feel the excitement running from my body to hers and back again, little shivers of our shoulders and backs and legs.

We should've brought the flashlight, I said. But no, Jean said, the candle is nice. The flame was shaped like a teardrop, fiery and orange, with blue at the bottom. The blue was almost invisible because it was so dark. It was dark under the porch, and also because it was night, after one o'clock in the morning. We were waiting for Jean's father to come.

I wish we had a Ipod, Jean said. She was always wishing for things. I wish we had a Kit Kat, she said, or even some Now & Laters. I had some Smarties in my pocket and I rolled over to get them and then I fed them to her one by one with my fingers. Her mouth and her tongue were warm. If we had a Ipod, somebody would be able to hear it, I said. Not if we had earbuds, she said back. Then we lay quiet for a while, listening to the wind scuffling around in the dead leaves. I wondered how long those leaves had been under there. I thought it might be practice for being dead, lying there in the dark with the dirt and the dead leaves. I didn't say this to Jean, she doesn't like that kind of stuff. She would say to stop being creepy.

I had never met Jean's father, even though I had known her for so long. He didn't live at home anymore. I knew her mother, who drank. She was foreign, she didn't speak English very well. She had an accent – not one of the kind that are supposed to be sexy but one of the thick kind. For a long time when I first knew Jean, she never invited me over to her house. I wasn't upset about this. We saw each other at school, and after school, and when we skipped school. Jean came over to my house sometimes but not usually. And then, finally, I went over there because Jean had my baseball cap, an old Indians one. It wasn't so much that I needed it, but I wanted it. I could have waited and asked her to bring it to school, but I wanted to get it from her. I wanted to get it from her hand. I wanted maybe to stand in her room and watch her take it out from wherever it was, her dresser drawer or under her bed. This was before we had sex, but not too long before.

So I went over there and Jean's mother opened the door. She looked different, not like my mother. She wore her hair in a bun, like old women do, and her dress looked different. She was drinking something out of a glass that she had on the kitchen table. Who are you, she said. I'm Matt, I said. She sat down at the table and stared at me, not saying anything else. The stuff in the glass was whiskey. I could tell, even though I had never tasted whiskey then. Jean has my baseball cap, I said. She looked at me and didn't answer. I started to wonder if I was in the right house. Maybe she didn't even know Jean. Maybe it was like some book I had read and Jean had been space-warped away from her house and every trace of her existence wiped out. No one even remembered her name, except me. Jean, Jean, I thought, remembering, and then she came into the room. She had wanted to get a glass of milk, she said to me later, and didn't even know I was there. I thought she might be mad at me, especially since her mother was acting so weird. I thought how she'd never invited me to her house and here I was butting in. I didn't even know then that her mother drank.

Her mother is used to me now, though. When I come over she doesn't even notice most of the time. Sometimes she makes us something to eat or else we make our own. Sometimes she talks to me about where she came from. She will be talking in her bad English, waving her hands, and then she'll be talking in her old language. She doesn't even notice the difference. If Jean and I aren't doing something I sit there and listen for a while. She's OK, Jean's mother. Her father is another story, according to Jean.

What if he doesn't come, I said. We'll come back some other time, Jean said. What if he never comes, I said. He'll come, she said. I know him. I don't know what you think we're doing here, I said. But in a way I did. The Smarties had made me hungry and I rolled around trying to see if there was anything left in my pockets. There hadn't been anything for dinner at Jean's house because her mother was passed out upstairs. There were some cold cabbage things stuffed with rice but they looked gross so we didn't have any. There would have been food at my house, but I was supposed to be sleeping over at Josh's house and so I couldn't go home. We had gone to McDonald's but we only had enough money for a small fries. In the inside pocket of my jacket I found a cough drop. We took turns sucking on it. I remember my mother giving me cough drops, I told Jean. When I had a sore throat she used to come in the night and give me a cough drop. She'd sit by me until it was all gone so I didn't choke. My mother doesn't even know what a cough drop is, Jean said. The cough drop got thin, as thin as paper, and we passed it back and forth between our mouths, like kissing.

We had actually had sex only one time. I wasn't so sure I wanted to, but Jean said we should. It wasn't that I didn't want to, but I wasn't sure if I knew how. I knew all about getting excited and getting hard, but then what? I knew it was supposed to go someplace, I was supposed to put it someplace, but did you do it with your hand or was there some other way? Also I was afraid for Jean to look at me. But it turned out we did it in the dark. That had been two weeks ago. Both of us said we wanted to do it again, but we hadn't yet. Now, under the porch, would have been a good time if it wasn't that we were waiting for her father to come. When the cough drop was gone we kissed some more, moving around on the ground in the dead leaves trying to get comfortable. I wanted Jean to take off her blouse but she wouldn't. I began to get mad. What the hell are we doing here anyway, I said.

Jean was blowing little puffs of breath at the candle to make the flame wiggle. You know why, she said. What if he doesn't come, I said. He comes here every night, she said. Almost every night. He stays here. I knew all this. Her father was going with the woman who lived in the house, this house with the porch. He had left Jean's mother, who was now drinking. Although her father was foreign, he wanted an American woman, someone who spoke good English and dressed in a sexy way. He spoke English very well, according to Jean. You could hardly tell he wasn't born here. Sometimes I thought that Jean had an accent, just a little. I liked it, but she hated it when I said anything about it. I even liked the way her mother talked, except when she was so drunk that she started to yell. Yelling in a foreign language is worse than in English.

What are you going to do if he comes, I said. *When* he comes, Jean said. You don't have to do anything, she said.

Did you tell Karyn we had sex, I said. Karyn was her best friend, except for me. No, I didn't, Jean said. Karyn wouldn't understand. Understand what, I said. She just wouldn't understand, Jean said, so there was no point. I lay there in the dead leaves thinking that Jean meant that Karyn would be grossed out if she knew we'd had sex. Karyn was in the Mission Club at school. I guessed there wouldn't be any point, but still I thought that Jean might have told her.

Tell me a story, Jean said. She said this a lot. Usually I could think of something. I would tell her like about when we went on vacation to Cincinnati and Dayton, where my folks had relatives. I would tell her things I used to do when I was little, like trying to make a train in the basement with folding chairs. But now, under the porch, I couldn't think of anything. Come on, Jean said, tell me something. She wiggled closer to me and put her tongue in my mouth and moved it all around, over my teeth and under my tongue where it's soft, and as far back as she could get it, back in my throat. Come on, she said, with her tongue in and out of my mouth. Tell me.

I tried to kiss her some more but she wouldn't. OK, I said. I lay on my back with my arms behind my head. Looking up I could see the bottom of the porch, the little slits between the boards where light came through, the light from the street light. OK, once there were these two kids named Jean and Matt, I said. Not about Jean and Matt, Jean said. At least give them different names. OK, I said, it's Melinda and Jack. Jack is a name I would like for my own. Not Melinda, said Jean. OK, Natalie and Jack. Yes, Jean said. She lay on her back beside me. She took my hand and put it on her stomach.

There were Natalie and Jack, I said. They went to school but they were so smart they didn't need to do homework. Their teachers let them take all the time off they wanted to, as long as they took the tests at the end. They would only come to school to hang out with their friends, but only if they felt like it. Natalie was very, very beautiful.

I stopped to think what to say about Natalie. What did girls want to be said about them? Natalie was very beautiful, I said again. She and Jack wanted to be rich and famous when they grew up. They thought they would be doctors. Not doctors, Jean said. Too bloody. OK, I said, they wanted to be rock stars. Natalie was going to be the singer and Jack would play the bass guitar. They were going to move to California and live in a house in Malibu or someplace.

I don't know, Jean said. This is too much like some kind of stupid movie. All right, fine I said. Tell your own if you don't like it. But right then her father came. At first we didn't know it was him. But there was a car and then a car door slamming. Someone was walking up the steps. Shhh, Jean said. We were half kneeling, on our hands and knees in the dead leaves. We could hear voices. It was Jean's father and he was talking to someone. I could recognize his voice from when he talked to Jean on the phone. She would hold the phone to my ear when he was talking a lot. It was a loud voice, lower than my father's. His accent was like Jean's mother's but not as much.

"Don't be a child," he said to someone who answered right back, a woman. "I will if I want to," she said in a regular voice, American I mean.

It's her, Jean said. I knew she meant the woman he was going with. I nodded even though Jean couldn't see me. I put my mouth up against her ear and said what are we going to do. She didn't answer.

I could hear their feet on the floorboards. They were almost over our heads. They were moving a little but not walking, more as if they were rocking back and forth. They weren't saying anything. Then the woman laughed. She laughed and then stopped as if someone had put something in her mouth. They were kissing, I thought. He had put his tongue in her mouth.

I wished I was somewhere else. Jean's father was talking again in a low voice but I couldn't understand what he was saying. The woman didn't answer, but she sighed. I looked at Jean. I could see a slice of her face in the light that came through the floorboards. She was looking up as if she could see through the porch floor. Her lips were moving. Come on, she said. I got up. I thought she meant it was time to go, to go out and talk to her father. But she started to unzip my pants and pull them down.

Jean, I said to her, whispering. But she was pulling our shirts up and sliding the skin of her tits against my chest. The candle fell over and went out. Jean moved her lips up my neck to my mouth so I opened it and kissed her. Don't make a noise, she said in my ear when I started to groan. But the leaves were breaking and crackling under us.

"What's that noise?" the woman said, over our heads. "It's only a cat," Jean's father said in his rumbling voice.

Jean pulled away from me. I could feel a wet place on my leg. She was crawling away to the other end of the porch where we had got in. There was a broken place there, where I had scratched my arm. I could see the dark shape of her for a minute, and then she was out. Now she's going to do it, I thought. She's going to talk to her father. I knew I should go with her. But I felt funny, just like the other time we had sex, although we hadn't actually had sex this time. It was like when I had fall-

en on the playground once and hit my head. My head and my body felt
light, and I had to close my eyes and just rest for a minute.

Over my head there was a scuffling sound and a shout. "Who's
there?" Jean's father yelled. There was a sound of glass breaking, and
something heavy falling on the boards over my head. The woman
screamed. I was pulling my pants up and trying to run out from under
the porch. I hit my head getting through the broken place, and I fell out
into the yard. I stood up to see where Jean was. She was running down
the street, I could see her just going around the corner. The woman
looked across the porch and saw me and screamed again. "I'll call the
police!" she screamed at me. "Do you hear me? The police." I was afraid
to look away from her. The ground was lumpy and hard. I could see that
the storm door behind them was broken and there was broken glass
from it on the porch floor. The woman was standing in it, not screaming
anymore, the glass in shiny triangles all around her feet. Jean's father
was crouched over, still ducking, with his hands held up to his head. He
started to look up and I ran.

Running after Jean, I felt cold. It seemed too light outside, almost as bright as in the day. I could see Jean ahead running for the
schoolyard. My breath was hurting my throat but I ran faster. It was the
way you used to run when you were a little kid, how you ran as fast as
you could, just for the hell of it.

Jean was under the bleachers, kneeling on the gravel. I stood
next to her. Why is it so light out here, I said. She had her head down,
and she was bending over like she was going to be sick, but I saw that
she was laughing. What happened, I said. She shook her head. The ends
of her hair touched the ground, falling long over her face and shoulders.
I could see her skin under her hair and it was very white. I put my hand
on her back and I could feel her laughing through her bones.

I threw a rock at him but I only broke the door, Jean said. He
was scared, don't you think? I sat down and put my arm around her.
What a baby, Jean said. Don't you think he's a baby?

Why is it so light out here, I said. Jean laid her head against my
arm. Silly, it's the moon, she said. The moon must be shining. She held
her hand out into the white light so that it made a shadow on the gravel.

It was nothing, that little move, but it was just like her. I had known her for such a long time.

ON NOT HAVING CLEANED THE HOUSE

Once the house was new and had the cleanness of new yellow wood, pipes as shiny as mirrors, jewels of nuts and bolts holding parts together as if they were something to be worn. Paint lay on the walls like a caress of green, of blue. In the attic, birds looked in the windows, pecking against the glass in their envy, they slid on the slated slope of the roof, their claws clicking as they contemplated the chimney, its red bricks new-fired.

In its youth there was a baby who lived there and slept in one of the tiny bedrooms, the one with the wallpaper that was like stars, or the other blooming with yellow flowers. The baby was one of several probably, teased and nursed and cossetted and ignored by three brothers and sisters or five, the baby crawling on the floor among their socked and booted feet, picking up bits of lint from the maroon rug with its great ghostly white flowers, its knees a little grubby which its mother wouldn't notice until she picked it up to take it to the kitchen for lunch, mashed potatoes, mashed peas, shredded meat, crumbs of bread rubbed into the wood of the table. And they all crowded in after the mother and the baby, eating lunch at the same time, dropping crumbs of their sandwiches onto the floor where they worked their way into the cracks, where they stayed for a hundred years, sleeping like Sleeping Beauty. The baby would have had these five or seven brothers and sisters, but would be missed when it died as if it were the only one, its photograph taken in death as if it were a prince or a princess, in its best dress, white lace and silken bonnet strings. In the photo, which lay in the depths of the house, the baby is sitting propped up against a window, in the dining room where the western sun streams in the afternoon. Its arms are crossed in its lap, its eyes are closed against the streaming of the light, its eyelashes like lace against its tiny petal cheeks. This photograph lay in the house for a hundred years, flattening itself, curling slightly at the edges, hiding at the back of the linen closet drawer. For a hundred years, no one tidied it or swept it up or dusted it.

It's not that I didn't learn how to dust. Every Saturday afternoon I dusted, in one hand a soft rag that had been a diaper or towel or old shirt, my mother's emissary into the land of housekeeping. I leaned, swooning, over the long smooth sweep of the dining room table. The carved glass knobs of the china cabinet fit into my hands like the knob of a scepter. My dust-clothed fingers knew the folds and wrinkles of the old woman carved in wood, forever sitting and making lace on top of our bookcase. This was the field of Saturday afternoon, the mossy carpet under my feet, the wooden forest of furniture. Each week, invisibly, the dust had returned to manifest itself on the dust cloth like the stigmata.

In the house there is a secret place where the past can be turned like the pages of a book. Upstairs, first room on the right, in the closet, back left corner, can't miss it. Against the baseboard the wallpaper is loose and comes away from the wall like a fan. Who was it who liked this abstract design, hard little chips of color? Who covered up the cherry blossoms endlessly falling down the wall like pink snow? At bottom is the kind of plaster that has hair in it, hair combed from the manes of horses standing patiently to let their bodies be useful one last time.

When the old woman lived here she moved from room to room as if there were a path known only to her. Her feet touched the floors softly, softly on the wood, softly the carpet's worn white flowers, softly the old brown linoleum, as if she were an Indian in the forest disturbing not even a leaf. The light from the windows streamed in as she found her way, the softness of each step raising glowing motes of dust. The chairs in the kitchen salute her, three of them or five. She rubs her dish cloth over the table, pressing, scrubbing one more time the grain of the wood.

If it has darkened over the years, how can she tell? In the basement the tap drips, each drop the tick in a slow clock. The stone floor has heaved like the ocean, but slowly, so that a marble set down anywhere will roll away to live in a corner. In the back, one last jar of canned tomatoes sits on a shelf, a relic of the old garden.

I threw away the plastic flowers when I moved in, with plastic I could be ruthless. I threw away the old phone, as heavy as an anvil. The couch shaped like a boat, like a coffin, crouched on the tree lawn for a few days, as if someone might go out to sit on it, as if there might be a need, there by the street, for extra seating. But with the family of shot glasses I was more tender. Although I no longer go to church, I could not throw away the small holy water font with an angel's head.

There is the scrubbing of the kitchen floor, the wiping of the woodwork. There is the cleaning of the stove, of the sink with sharp grains of cleanser, the washing of the windows. There is the moving through the house with a dust mop, which anyone might do, the dust mop that is like a small hairy animal. When it is shaken outside, what escapes? This continual moving over the surfaces of the house, this slow friction of hand and cloth, a woman's hand, the cloth that was once the baby's blanket – what does it mean? The baby's mother moved her hand more and more slowly, watching the fading pictures flow over the wood, the smiling teddy bear, the rocking horse, the small blue scallops at the edge, now ragged. When her hand stopped, she stood there until the other children came home from school, banging their books on the floor with a thump.

Standing at the windows looking out, the yard and the street and the other houses move in a slow swirl, the grave pacing of walkers on the sidewalk speeded up like an old movie, always moving to the corner, the trolley stop, the bus, the little store where milk is sold, to school, to their job at the telephone company where even in the depression there is work, to the shoe repair store, to the dry cleaners owned by an old Hungarian woman who is dying among the chemical-stiff clothing. She is going to sell her business to a black couple who will join the church under protests, which will die away. From the windows the movement outside is a skein of lines, almost visible, crossing and recrossing. A cloth may be pressed against the windows, wiping. Once the windows were soft, the glass like sheets of candy, gleaming like water, but they have hardened now, nothing passes through. (The blue cleaner squirting from its bottle can never wipe away the mark of the tape that held up the Christmas decorations, put there incautiously by a child's hand, a red and green construction-paper Christmas tree, pointy, rough-edged.) From the windows, standing, looking out, wiping your hands on your apron, your jeans, resting your head against the glass, so hard now and cool against the skin, you can watch the birds fly across the sky, almost too fast to see, the leaves as small as a squirrel's ear, growing large, turning red, turning brown.

Birds come into the house because they love it, large cave, roofed with stone, pillars as white as cream. They wriggle in under the eaves, fly down the chimney. Inside they are bewitched, slaves to the dark, to the unfairness of the ceiling. They scrabble at the unhappy enchantment of windows, trying to remember how to fly through clear spaces, how to soften the slabs of air. If there is a man who knows how, he can catch them in his hands, where they lie without fluttering, their eyes soft and bright. He can put them in the old birdcage and set it on the kitchen table for a surprise. When they have danced and sung for the children who are left, he can take them to the porch and let them fly from his palms. But if they must, they die there, they lie in the basement by the furnace, behind the hot water heater, for a hundred years, their wings sodden bits of fluff, their bones flattening. When they are found, they ride the flat bed of the old spade outside.

If the children have gone, are there still dolls here? Is there still a wagon rusting in the basement, a sled? Does the old metal bed that slept three ring when the breeze from the open door moves through its springs?

On moving day, the old furniture met the new, stiffly, politely, no reason to make a scene. Crowded in like a family of immigrants, they crouched together, making the best of things. A path had to be made for the living, a route to walk to the alarm, to the cup of coffee, the toast. At night, the cupboards revealed their treasures: a yellow vase, a box made from popsicle sticks, four marbles in a small glass jar. Yes, there is the photo, yes the baby is still dead. The brothers and sisters of the baby have grown up, they live in another photo where they sit around the kitchen table with glasses in their hands, and also in Florida. The furniture has to wait in the depot of the dining room for a long time while places are found. One chair, one lamp at a time moves out to populate the house. Here, the sewing table, here the cushion with a picture of a cat on it. On the wall, the photo of the new family's ancestors, nineteenth-century faces looking into the twentieth. Sitting on the couch that did not go out to the lawn, I felt disquiet. I felt the old paths of the house under my feet, the ghosts of the old furniture. Who would I meet in the morning when I came down the stairs, whose hand still rummaged among the plastic flowers, looking for a photo? For a long time, the house was stiff around me, hardened.

The children would sit, twittering like birds, to hear the stories of the princess who is kissed, the princess who sleeps behind barbed roses, the prince who is turned into a swan, who climbs up a ladder of hair. In the long evenings of winter, snow falling outside the windows which were slowly growing harder, icier, at the sunny bedtimes of summer, sunburned legs restless on the sheets. One would need a glass of water, one a handkerchief, one a doll dressed all in plaid like a Scotsman. The doll had a purse but it is long gone, lost, laid to rest in the closet with the winter clothes. The purse is bent and dusty, but still holds a single penny. Three in a bed, their heads like the knobs of clothespins above the sheet, they yawn, fighting sleep, for who knows how long it will be before they wake? They have prayed, yes, but they remember the baby who has not come back. The baby was kissed by their mother who is as beautiful as a princess, by their father the prince, but still, still she slept. Downstairs, the lamp is glowing.

Outside the house, dust is falling from the stars, the dust of a hundred suns is sifting down, through the boards, through the cracks. The dark sky is lying on the roof, the stars press against the slates.

In the afternoon when I might clean I sit looking out the windows. I have a dream in my head of cleaning, of the starched apron, the pearls, the shirtwaisted dress. I know the romance of the full larder, the gleaming dishes, the silverware kept in a felted box, the dance of the broom, the vacuum cleaner – for they were revealed to me by my mother. Feather dusters, embroidered dish towels, jars of shell-shaped soaps; a cocktail with a cherry in it, the glass as clear and hard as if made of ice. I learned to iron, the hot heaviness gliding under my hand, the sharp smell of crisped, not quite burned cloth rising to my nose like the rarest perfume. But when I reach out my hand, all this is gone. I am thinking of the marble in the corner, of the bird lying on the basement floor.

I tell myself that dust is not negligible. When it swirls in the streams of sun it is as beautiful as gold, and if we cannot spend it, all the better. When it lies in the accumulation of years it is as furry as a loved animal. It is light, volatile, it flies through the air like a swarm of microscopic birds. The stripe of dust I might wipe up with a gloved finger is not dirt: these are cosmic particles, stony bits of the Acropolis, the transfigured flecks of skin and hair that may have belonged to heroes, saints, lovers, children, babies not yet a year old who could walk and speak a few words as well as anyone.

When the baby died, yes, they were sad. Yes, the baby's things were put away in a drawer and the mother, her beautiful princess eyes wet and red, would open the drawer when no one was at home to look at the little shirts, the dress with real lace, the bonnet that the baby had never liked to wear. The baby had pushed the bonnet away, not caring that it had flowers on it, yellow flowers as lovely as if they were alive. The baby's mother couldn't help but think of this, of the baby pushing the bonnet off, when she was making dinner for the other three or five children, when her hands were busy with the vegetables, putting out bowls of cherries, of grapes, cutting quick slices of cake, equal in size from the eldest to the youngest. The vision of the baby's hand pushing the bonnet off was always before her for a while, and also how the baby in the picture let the bonnet lie against her forehead, never caring, never lifting a hand, how the bonnet strings lay across her chest, their bow perfect and even. Even when she started to forget, the bow stayed with her, the silken strings in their loops. She dreamed them for years, dreamed them when as an old woman she walked the paths of the house, her hands touching the furniture, for support and for comfort. Dreamed them when she stood looking out the windows as the birds flew quickly past, the cars in a slow stream down the street. Dreamed them in Florida where she lay in her nursing home bed that the eldest son had found for her. When he came to visit on Wednesdays and Sundays, she would listen to him talk without answering, her hand restless on the sheets, the perfectly tied bow always before her.

Monday was washing day, yes and Saturday for baking, but the other days? It was easy to forget.

The house is crumbling, has always been crumbling. Since the beginning: deep in the house are secret caches of sawdust that sifted from the hands of the builders. Each year of its life is marked by the long slow shift that is the house transforming itself into dust, dust falling like snow, like the pink snow of cherry blossoms. The light streams through the windows of the dining room each afternoon notwithstanding, soft sun on the windows, on the reconciled furniture. The birds fly past, weaving a net about the house that is fine but as strong as steel. The crumbs sleep in the cracks, among the flowers of the carpet. If the basement tap drips, it cannot be heard. When I move through the house, I am as silent as I can be, my foot meeting the floor with the softness of a caress, so as not to disturb the movement of the golden dust that spirals in the air. The windows are made of looking-glass and in them I can see many things. I am wearing the house like a garment. I am leaving myself here, swept into the corners, rolling into cracks, rubbed into the wood of the furniture like the purest, finest oil. I am looking for a marble, a photo, the plaid purse whose penny I can spend. At night when I cannot sleep I will fill the holy water font, I will go out into the night and lie on the old sofa, the boat sofa, and watch the house for a hundred years as roses grow over it, soft petals closing the eyes of its windows, sharp thorns at the door.

TRANSUBSTANTIATION

Here we are, and it's nice that we're together. We are sisters. We may be dead. I'm not sure I want to clear up the question, for what good would it do to know? We might have to take action of some sort, and there are no instructions, no help of any kind on offer.

How appropriate that it seems to be a coffee house. A place where coffee is served and you can sit for hours. Is it still called that? Time may have passed, things may have changed. My position was always that I was au courant, on top of things. My sister said no to change. But she had a cell phone. It was only a no in principle.

She purses her lips. She knows I'm thinking this. She can read my mind. But this has nothing to do with being dead, if we are, because we could always do this in an unreliable way. "Are we dead?" I ask her. "What do you think?"

She refuses to answer. She doesn't like to be wrong, or out of control. She likes to steer, metaphorically but also literally. There is a family story that we were in a canoe, placed there by our well-meaning parents, who always thought we were going to turn out to be more active or athletic or competent than we were. A canoe—anyone can do it. An idiot can paddle a canoe. I was twelve and she was nine. By chance I was put in the end of the canoe where you have to steer. The bow? the stern? both ends looked the same.

The lake was small, flat, nearly waveless, except for the thrashing started up by other canoers. There was no question of drowning, or almost none. Our mother stood on the dock mak ing exaggerated paddling motions with her arms, digging great scoops in the air. She called instructions to us, but even without having done much we had floated far enough away that we couldn't hear her anymore. Or didn't want to. She was wearing a coral blouse, new then, which she wore until it was a rag and beyond that, finally letting it end its days in picking up dust in tandem with a can of Pledge.

We were alone in the canoe, making feeble stabs at the water with our paddles, moving out into the middle where, we knew, something fearful waited. How deep was it, we asked each other. My sister has a good head for facts, but this one had eluded her. Twenty feet? fifty? How deep was fifty feet? We've never been good at spatial thinking, and we had to imagine fifty feet as a series of six-foot men (our father) stacked on each other, head to foot, the bottommost one standing on the floor of this lake, the eighth with his head still two feet below the water. I imagined I could see his head under the waves, its hair (sparse, like our father's) lifting away from the scalp, and said so, but my sister rebuked me. "You cannot," she said, and of course she was right.

It was somewhat like being dead, out there on the middle of the lake, with no idea how to get back. No idea how to turn the canoe around, or how to steer it in any direction at all. That is, if we are in fact dead.

My sister recommends that we make a list. She is the practical one. We don't have pens or paper, so it has to be a mental list.

First, are we dead? Find out.

Is there any place else besides this?

If dead, how did we die?

Do either of us by any chance have a candy bar?

It's a short list, but we are pleased with it. "Did we die on that lake?" I ask, even though I know we didn't.

"Don't be silly," she says. We laugh.

I know we didn't because I have all the memories of what came after. Not just the memory of being towed in, and other people laughing, and our mother explaining how we'd never been in a canoe before, but everything after that. My decision not to play at dolls with my sister anymore, high school, dating a boy just because he was taller than me, my job at a bank where my boss came on to me, early marriage, being pregnant in giant, elastic-waisted blue jeans, dying my hair for the first time, my decision to go on estrogen, all that and more.

Of course, as my sister points out, these could be false or implanted memories. It could be a construct of the mind in the moment of death, as Swedenborg theorized. The mind can't accept its dissolution, and so creates a world of memories in an instant, furnishing a life with elastic and Miss Clairol Auburn and coin-counting machines. But why wouldn't I make up a better life for myself, I say to her. Why let my hair go gray? Why would a twelve-year-old think of estrogen?

"Maybe the canoe itself is false," she says. "Did you think of that?"

I don't want to let go of the canoe, and I hug to myself its curves, its shabby green color, the puddle of murky water that had gathered in its lowest point. Our parents had grown small. From the center of the lake, they were no bigger than half my finger. "We were empowered," I say to her. "It was the beginning of adulthood."

"See how well that's turned out," she says. She gets bitter when she's feeling depressed, and I squeeze her fingers.

"I wonder if there is any coffee," I say, to distract her. I don't drink coffee anymore, because of my jumpy heart, but if we are dead, maybe I could tolerate it. If there is any coffee. If the dead drink.

The coffee house is dusty, disheveled. The chairs are pulled out as if everyone else got up and left a minute ago, in a hurry to go someplace else. There are empty cups here and there, and crumpled napkins.

"We could write on the napkins," she says, and I know she is thinking of the list, but there are no pens that we can see.

There is a display case on one side, the kind that showcases pastries, but there are no pastries in it. It's empty except for a flashlight, a wooden statue, and a few paperback books, which I am glad to see. I hate to go anywhere without reading material.

The coffee house has two doors, one to our left, one behind the counter where a cash register should be but isn't. An espresso machine hulks on the other side of the counter, rusty and ancient. There are no windows, and even though this seems like a minus, I am glad. I don't want to know just yet what might be outside these walls.

"Isn't this ironic?" I say to my sister. "A coffee house with no coffee."

"Just as well," she says. "It's not very sanitary." She runs her finger across the table and shows me the fur of dust it has picked up. Fastidiously, she wipes her hand on one of the napkins and brushes at her skirt to remove invisible motes. She has always dressed better than me, wears skirts more often, often an accent scarf at her neck, earrings even on ordinary days. It used to be that I had better hair to make up for it, but this advantage waned as my hair got grayer, more wiry, and finally started falling out. Unless this is a false memory. Maybe I have never had to resort to Rogaine, 2% strength for women. Maybe my hair is still luxuriant and well behaved. But where would this docile and beautiful hair be, in what universe or plane of existence? It's enough to give me a headache.

"So," I say with the air of one planning a campaign, "are we dead?"

"I remember a hospital," my sister says hesitantly. "Beeping, machines, a nurse with teddy bears on her scrubs. A purple vase of carnations falling on the floor?"

"I remember that, too," I said, "but that was when Dad was in with his broken hip."

"So, not us."

"Unless it's a false memory," I say. Which takes us back to the canoe. Just as then, we are indecisive. We look around the coffee house as we looked around the lake, wanting something to hold on to, something to give context. I remember thinking in the canoe that perhaps if I had been a better girl, more religious, better behaved in school with the nuns, that I could have walked over the water. I thought about trying. I thought I might be able to figure it out and teach my sister. It would have taken only a few minutes to walk back to the dock if we got the trick of it. I remember putting my hand in the water, testing its firmness.

"We knew how to swim," my sister says, and this time it seems more strange that she has read my mind. The air seems more elastic, a little gelatinous, a fit medium for thoughts. We did know how to swim.

"I didn't like the look of the water," I tell her, and she nods. The water was opaque, unlike the translucent blue water of the swimming pool at the Y where we had lessons, where you could see the black lines on the bottom marking the lanes. The water in the lake was dark green, bottomless. There were probably fish in it, and we had no truck with fish, no desire to know them more intimately. If we had had to swim back to shore, we would have stayed in the boat until the lake dried up, until the glaciers crept back and engulfed us with ice, until the atmosphere lifted off and was sucked into space by the close approach of a black hole.

I had told her at the time of my plan to walk across the water, and she had pretended to consider it. We both pretended. Our parents seemed so far away by then that they might as well have died and been reincarnated into a new life which was being lived out on dry land, leaving us behind in a watery world, furnished by a water bottle and a discarded pair of sunglasses in the bottom of the canoe. We had one Snickers bar squashed into my sister's pocket, which she divided fairly by biting it in half.

The memory of the Snickers bar made me hungry. Do the dead hunger? It seemed that they might, and even though I hadn't eaten a Snickers bar for years, I longed for one. "Do you remember the Snickers?" I said, and she nodded. Later, we always ate Snickers bars when we got high—the inrush of dope made a space in the brain that was exactly fitted for caramel, nougat, peanuts, chocolate.

I got up and went behind the counter, driven by this candy vision, and started going through the drawers and cupboards.

"Is there anything?" she asked. I shook my head, even as I opened more doors, peered into the backs of more shelves. A few coffee filters, some ancient crumbs, a mouse trap, still unsprung. Nothing interesting or useful.

"Are we dead?" she asked, and I didn't know what to say. If we were, it seemed like such a pointless kind of death. (Although wasn't death always pointless?) And boring. I went to the display case to check out the paperbacks. There were three: a horseracing mystery, a Zane Grey, and a novel by someone named Wilson. I brought them back to the table, and we examined them, but if they held clues, we couldn't figure out what they meant. They had been read hard. Corners of the pages were bent back, the covers soft and worn. Wilson's book was falling apart, the pages would have scattered like leaves if we had taken less care. The pages were stained, as if they had gotten wet and dried out imperfectly.

The Zane Grey made me nostalgic. I had read a number of them the year I was eleven, the year of the canoe. I had imagined myself on a horse, riding hard to someone's rescue. I had imagined myself in the canyon with a man who loved me. "Roll the stone, Lassiter," I had imagined myself saying as Jane does at the end of *Riders of the Purple Sage*. This vision of myself as heroic had taken a hit from the canoe incident, for not only did it turn out that I couldn't walk on water, couldn't rescue my sister, couldn't even turn the damn canoe around, but I had to be rescued myself, and not romantically by a good looking slightly older boy who might ask if I was doing anything later after my parents had gone to sleep in our mildewed cabin, but by the park manager, who was bald and red-faced and really mad at us. I had sometimes dreamed about him as I got older, those unhappy dreams where the world skews around you and there are spiders under the rugs, and your husband won't vacuum them up, but pretends they aren't there.

"We were married, right?" I said to her.

"I believe so," she said, as if considering it, as if remembering something that had taken place a long time ago. "If it was not a dream."

When we were in the canoe, we had already thought of marriage, of course. We had bride paper dolls, and we married them off to stuffed animals or the Indian doll in his fake leather and feathers. We expected we'd be married, but it would happen in a different country. We hadn't learned the language yet. We knew we had to go to high school first and perhaps to Niagara Falls, which was always promised but never happened. Our father's vacation was always too short. By the time we married, we would be someone else, and this turned out to be true. "Did we have children?" my sister said.

"We might have," I said, hedging even though I remembered children. I didn't want to bring them here, not even in a memory. Not even in a memory that might be false or created. The only children we had here were the two of us in the canoe, in the middle of the lake, on the dark water. We drank the water in the bottle, we ate the Snickers bar. We took turns trying on the sunglasses. We described our clothes to each other, pretending we were models. In the distance, people called. Cars zoomed on the highway far away. Picnickers sat at their tables on the shore and ate out of coolers. Our future husbands might well have been there, our employers, the beautician who dyed my hair orange when I distinctly told her dark red, the man at the bank who always pretended he didn't remember my sister although she'd come there a hundred times. The librarian who saved books for me, the neighbor who was a minister and insisted on talking to my sister when she only wanted to go into the house and pour a glass of wine.

Had we gotten into a car that day? Had someone wrapped blankets around us even though we weren't wet? Had someone called the ambulance? Did my head rest uncomfortably on the stony ground? Did my sister's hand lie limp across her chest, showing the bitten-away vacation nail polish?

The lake, the beautiful, possibly false, implanted lake lay across my memory, its sheen bright and blinding, its depths unfathomable. The canoe floated hesitantly on it, like a leaf or a scrap of light. When we put our hands in the water they looked greenish, translucent, and we snatched them up because they seemed ready to float away, hardly a part of ourselves anymore. When we bent over to see our reflections, we looked older, our hair darkened, our eyes filled with knowledge.

I took my sister's hand. "We are dead," I said to her, because I was the eldest and a decision had to be made.

GOING TO MOONVILLE

In the car it was steamy, smoky. The heat on and off, on and off, the windows rolled up, then cracked, the smoke from Roger's cigarette flowing out in a thin stream. The stuffiness was the kind that made Evie carsick, the warm queasy air pressing on her. She could remember riding the bus to school and feeling just as she did now, that stale feeling in your stomach. The roads wound round and round, up and down hill, the fields beside them rising and falling until she had no idea where they were or what direction they were going. Moonville. I've been up there many times, Roger was saying. Used to go in high school, scare the girls, you know how it is.

Evie knew. Moonville. She didn't care so much if it was haunted or not. She didn't care about ghosts. What did they have to say that she wanted to hear? But she liked the sound of it, the idea of the moon. She liked the stories that went along with the ghosts—the lost town, the tunnel where the trains didn't run. She liked the past when it was a story, with people who were in love, not when it was history, dates listed in a book that would be on a test.

It's spooky up there, Roger said. Spooky but nice. He poked her, making her jump. I'll be there to protect you.

Evie laughed. She drank from her water bottle and opened the window again, letting her hand trail out on the side of the car, letting the wind chill her skin. It's getting cold, she said.

Roger put on the radio and started to sing along with Beyonce, acting silly, going off key on purpose, but Evie sighed. She was bored. It was spring again and she was still here, small town girl going nowhere. She'd started seeing Roger mainly because he was older. It was interesting that he was married. She'd seen his pale-skinned wife around, coming out of Kroger's with a bag of groceries, or at Pizza Crossing. He had a truck which she'd liked at first, but all he wanted to do was go offroad in it. When you've seen one mudhole, you've seen them all. Moonville. Why not? Bring on the ghosts, she said to Roger, and he echoed her, Bring them on, baby.

The sky was blue, feathered with clouds, the sun sinking through the layers. All of southeast Ohio was sunk in green, pocked and seamed with ravines, threaded with streams, gleam of waterfalls showing through the leafing trees. When the glaciers came the ice had gone only so far and no farther, leaving the land they touched smooth and rolling, ready for fields of corn and soybeans. But southeastern Ohio, un-iced, was rough and rocky, hard farming, tiny fields in pockets of bottom land, squeezed between the hills. Good for rockclimbers, for rollercoaster roads, good for getting lost, good for ghosts.

Can I have a juice box?

When we get there, OK?

When will we get there? Can I have ice cream?

There is no ice cream there. We're going to walk in the woods, remember? We're going to Moonville.

Moonville, Taylor said after her father. Moonville. The moon lives in Moonville, right?

Not really.

Then why is it Moonville?

I don't know, he said, in such a way that she was quiet for a while. Taylor could see the moon in the sky, pale like it always was in the daytime, like a white dish on a tablecloth. She could put her finger over it if she wanted to. She had the idea that it was bigger than it looked. As big as a car or a house. You could live in it, or someone could, a man. Or maybe he lived in Moonville. The car bounced and shook her. Her seatbelt lay loose in her lap, it had lost its tightness. The trees rushing by made her eyes hurt, but she kept them open, looking for cows or a dog. Back a ways there had been baby lambs, a hundred of them at least, falling down a green hill with their mammas running after them.

Are there baby lambs in Moonville, Taylor asked.

Maybe there used to be.

They had gone away, Taylor thought. She was named after someone on tv, a soap opera, and so was her sister who had gone away. Her sister Brooke. You can say a prayer to your sister Brooke, her sitter was always telling her. She can watch out for you from heaven. But she didn't believe this, because Brooke had been a tiny baby when she left and she couldn't even sit up by herself. Her mother had gone away too, but not to heaven.

Where did they go? she asked, but her father didn't answer. She hadn't expected him to. Her doll Laurette was in her lap and she spoke into Laurette's ear. Moonville, moonville, moonville.

"From the Lake Hope dam and State Route 278, turn onto Hope-Moonville Road, stay to the left at the fork. The third time you cross the old railroad bed, you are at the abandoned town of Moonville…. Pull off where the berm widens just past the bridge. Walk the old railroad bed to the left, cross Raccoon Creek and Moonville Tunnel will be 100 yards straight ahead. The tunnel is no longer visible from the road. Be careful crossing Raccoon Creek during times of high water." Visitor Information Brochure, Lake Hope State Park.

Irene hesitated on the bank. The water was rushing past her feet with a febrile intensity, brown and opaque, the foam dirty beige. Above the crossing rocks, it pooled deeply, the color of dark beer, tiny rafts of leaves floating serenely. The rocks themselves were damp and some of them were mossy. She wanted to believe herself agile, lithe, someone who would think nothing of leaping from rock to rock, her hair flying behind her. But she had weak ankles and her back hurt. She felt the thickness around her middle, a weight that would hold her down. And her hair was too short now to fly. But—Moonville. It was on the

other side, and she had to go. Caidin was already halfway across, his
white fur wet to his shoulders. He looked back at her to see if she was
coming. People told her he wasn't very smart, but they didn't know him,
his sweetness, how he felt things. People being Ed, he ex-husband. He
had never liked Caidin, not his name, not his color. German Shepherds
weren't supposed to be white, he said.

The air was full of sound and message. Timidly, she set her foot
on the first rock, only a foot from the bank. It wobbled and she stepped
the other foot quickly across, then stood there frozen. Caidin barked
encouragement but her head was ringing, voices chiming one over the
other. If only they said sensible things, she thought. Meaningless sounds,
advertising jingles, lines of dialogue from sitcoms, things from the past.
Since her operation they never shut up. Don't sit on cement or you'll
get a chill down there and you'll never have babies--her mother's voice,
cracked and foggy from cigarettes. Who needed to hear that? She was
past worrying about babies. She had rechristened herself as an act of
healing: Irene, her middle name, although everyone still called her Betty.

The next rock was a little farther away, she'd have to stretch.
The water foamed around it with a sucking sound. Irene spent a little
time watching a branch still bearing green leaves come down river past
the gauntlet of the rocks. She had been here before, long ago, long ago.
Moonville. Prom night. Voices from twenty-seven years ago still hung in
the air. I dare you. I'll get my dress wet. Be careful of the beer. Her date
had carried her across, her red lace gown dragging in the water, her hair
streaming over his shoulder. She should have changed into shorts like
some of the other girls. She could feel the past like a spear through her
body, its spent potency rising in her and falling away. Bending her knees
for more spring, she leaned toward the next rock.

In the forest the trees leaned toward each other, the wind rising a little.
Green, they had to be green, their leaves had to grow toward the sun. Vines wove in the
branches, May apple umbrellas shaded the moss. Things were buried in the ground:
nuts, lost marbles, gum wrappers, small bones. Green the trees, silty brown the water.

Are we there?

We're almost there. Her father's hair was standing up at the back
of his head which made him look like Mr. Jim's rooster who lived in a

pine tree. Taylor was allowed to scatter his feed when she came through the hedge to visit. Mr. Jim used to work on the railroad, he had showed her his hat when he was the engineer. The rooster had another chicken for a friend and soon there would be chicks.

Laurette wants some juice, she said.

She'll have to wait for a goddamn minute.

You'll have to wait for a goddamn minute, Taylor said to Laurette, and her father laughed. Don't say that, he said. Don't listen to me.

There was nothing to look at, no houses, only the trees.

"At one time there were approximately 100 people living at Moonville. Moonville is thought to be named for a man called Moon who once operated a store in the town. Moonville is famous for two things: The Tunnel and the 'Moonville Ghost.'" Visitor Information Brochure, Lake Hope State Park.

Taylor put her hand on her father's thigh. He was wearing his old jeans and they were soft. She stroked it.

Don't do that baby girl. I'm driving.

Taylor made Laurette sit beside her, outside of the seatbelt. If there was an accident her head would hit the windshield and she would be dead, which meant gone. Laurette had hair the same color as Taylor, brown. Her body was hard plastic and her eyes opened and closed with a click. Her father had bought her at an auction for Taylor but she was as good as a new doll. Taylor closed Laurette's eyes with her finger and held them shut. She closed her own eyes. We're going to sleep, she said.

Taylor's father nodded his head. Go to sleep honey and we'll be there before you know it and then we'll have a picnic.

The picnic was juice boxes and Ritz crackers with American cheese and green olives and a Snickers bar to share and a bottle of beer for Taylor's father. They had packed it up in a bag from the Krogers. Got to get you out in the fresh air, her father had said. Get out of this poky old town, have a little fun. Taylor's father worked for the county which meant he got a dark tan. Taylor went to daycare or sometimes stayed with Aunt Amy who wasn't her aunt. Aunt Amy was fun except when she talked on the phone too much and then Taylor went out and played in her yard which wasn't the same as being out in the fresh air. Aunt Amy liked her father but he didn't like her as much. She talks too much, he told Taylor when she asked why not. He went out sometimes with a girl, but it wasn't anything serious. I'll be getting you a mamma sometime, he said to Taylor, but not just yet a while.

The car was slowing down, the car was stopping and Taylor stopped pretending to be asleep. Are we here? she said.

Almost, her father said. He took the bag and got out of the car and walked around to take Taylor's hand. There was nothing to see but more trees. Come on, he said and they started walking down a path which was just dirt. It's not far, he said. When Taylor looked back she could hardly see their car for all the green around it.

Why don't we just screw? Evie said. She'd gotten tired of the idea of Moonville.

That's in my plans. Roger was driving the car one-handed, and on each curve of the road Evie tensed as he went too close to the edge.

We want to go here, why? she said.

Just something to do, baby, someplace to be.

Someplace where they wouldn't run into his wife or someone who would tell her, as Evie knew. It was OK with her that he was married, but sometimes it was a pain. Why can't we go to Columbus, she said. We could stay in a motel and go out someplace.

There was no place in Logan to go, it was too small. No place she hadn't been before—five pizza places, a bookstore/coffee shop, the Mexican restaurant, Jack's Steakhouse. These were the kinds of places you went, and she was tired of them.

If we drove to Columbus right now we could go out to dinner and then go and have sex and be back by midnight. Which was when Roger said his wife was expecting him.

Couldn't make it before one, if that. Roger pulled the car onto the edge of the road.

Is this it? Evie looked around. There's nothing here.

We have to walk in, Roger said, but he didn't open the door. He reached over and ran his hand down over her nearest breast.

I'm tired of doing it in cars.

Come on Evie, give me a kiss. He hooked his other hand around her neck and tugged her forward. Take your seatbelt off. He kissed her cheek and put his big tongue in her ear.

Caidin whined on the bank, wanting her to hurry across. Irene crouched, her bottom resting against her heels. The water rushed around her, its glassy little waves sucking at her rock, breaking into little rills and ruffles of foam. She was in the middle, she was glad to see. Midriver, midlife. She might certainly live to be eighty or more, after all, in spite of everything. Her Granny Staples had made it to a hundred and three, dried up like an apple left at the back of a cupboard. When she touched Irene it was like a twig scratching at her, a shudder at the back of her neck. Betty she'd been then, of course. Irene put her hand in the water. So cold. How white her hand looked under the water, greenish-white, wavering, unsolid, as if she might begin to dissolve and float away. The weather was strange. Not quite summer, but the season seemed already to be winding down, the heat weak and flavorless. Caidin barked sharply, looking into the woods, toward Moonville

What is it? she called. He was standing stiffly, his legs braced. He was sensitive, she thought. He knew what there was to know in heaven and on earth. Her ankles ached, and her knees were building up pain. She'd have to stand soon or she'd fall when she did. If she fell, she'd slide into the pool just below her. She imagined her face underwater, lit by the greenish light down there, just as if she were looking at herself in an old mirror. Lying there, the cold of the river rocks at your back, the water rushing past you, lie there and wait for what comes, wait for boredom if that's what comes, wait until you see your way.

Caidin, she called, and he turned to her. Caidin, she said again, using the weight of his glance to pull herself up. Now, she said to herself, facing the rocks.

Some say that the ghost is a conductor who fell on the track and was decapitated. Some say the ghost was a young man on his honeymoon who in his marital exuberance leaned too far out the train window. His head bounced back into the lap of his new bride, his blood staining her going-away dress. Some say the ghost was a man who worked for the railroad and lived in Moonville. He left a family party to go down and walk in front of the train, no one knew why, and now he walks down to the train every evening, as punctual as if he were punching a time clock, as if the train still ran. Some say that the ghost is many ghosts, the remains of the living people who worked and sang and ate in Moonville, who are buried in the little Moonville cemetery. They're restless, these ancient Moonville citizens, uneasy in their earth beds, getting up at all hours to dance as orbs of light that can be captured by the cameras of amateur ghost hunters.

Irene lay against the bank sobbing. Caidin put his head against her and licked her cheek. Her ankle hurt and she had a long scratch down her arm from where she'd grabbed at a thorn bush to stop herself from falling in. Her pants were wet to the thighs. The incision over her ribs ached and she put her hand on it to quiet it. Why is it so hard? she asked Caidin, who barked in answer. He barked again, and she said yes, yes, I made it across, I know. Caidin always looked on the bright side. She pulled herself up to the grassy verge and sat, legs crossed. To calm herself, she closed her eyes and let her mind roam, letting loose of her self.

I am lying in the grass, she said, and saw her hand against the sky as if she could push it back and unroll it. I am surrounded by the grass, a small forest, one with the ants and the grasshoppers. The sky stretched over her tightly, covering her, pressing her into the earth. She could feel her body quieting, relaxing into the hollows and lumps of the stream bank, just as the visualization tape had said.

Then the moon, which was silver and dusty. The craters were filled with a litter of rocks and sand, the ground gritty under her feet. Was it called the ground on the moon? or was that a word that could only be used on earth? Caidin whined in her ear, and she patted him, without opening her eyes. The sky looked black but she knew it was a blue so dark that no one could tell the difference. The stars were hung in it like a forest of earrings, each one sparkling. The sun a hard ball of light.

She opened her eyes to the river, letting its amber pools and white foam be beautiful again, unmenacing. She was on the other side.

Now let's get up there, she said to Caidin. She wiped some mud from her hands, and then slapped her thigh, saying come on, come on boy. Above them the trestles loomed. The tracks had been taken away, and the trestles looked like Stonehenge, or so she preferred to think.

Evie could feel Roger shudder, and obligingly, she moaned and thrust her hips up. She'd come several minutes ago, neatly and quickly as she always did. She ran her hand down the back of his head, scratching his neck lightly with her fingernails, which he liked. Outside the car, she could see nothing but green, leaves and tree branches. A bird flew across the window and chirped. The feel of him sliding out of her was sort of nice, she thought, and she kissed the side of his head. He burrowed into the curve of her shoulder. Evie, Evie, he said. My God.

I think I hear somebody coming, she said. She wriggled out from under him and pulled her tank top down.

She'll be coming 'round the mountain when she comes, Taylor sang, her father chiming in. She'll be coming 'round the mountain she'll be coming 'round the mountain she'll be coming 'round the mountain when she comes. The path turned in circles, the trees marching by fast. That's a good old song, he said. Now where'd you learn that?

Aunt Amy taught me. She has it on a record.

Well, that's a good one.

Aunt Amy wanted to come, Taylor said.

Did she say that?

She said she'd make a picnic for us sometime.

She did, did she?

She said she'd make a pie.

Do you like Aunt Amy so much?

Taylor put her arms around Laurette and squeezed. She's OK, she said. I like pie.

Oh, everybody likes pie, don't you know? Everybody in the world or out of it, Taylor's father said. He sighed.

Brooke didn't like pie, Taylor said. She only liked milk. Don't you remember?

Her father didn't answer, and she squeezed Laurette harder, pushing her soft girl bones against Laurette's plastic. Laurette likes pie, she said, but her father still didn't say a thing.

This trail would have taken the Indians into prime hunting and wintering ground along Raccoon Creek.... I believe that this ancient "Buffalo Trace," as the old people in Vinton County named it to me, was abandoned after McArthurtown was established, c1815.... The trace down to the fording just above Moonville was very steep on both sides of Raccoon Creek. We know where the trail is on the north but haven't found it on the south side as it goes over the ridge and down to Pinney Hollow. oldeforester.com

Here, yes and over there, they had built fires, they had danced. Irene picked up a rock from the circle of a fire ring. She stood just in front of the tunnel, letting the voices wash over her, her mother, her father, her brother, her girlfriends. All dead now or married. Teeny gone to Columbus, Diane a nurse with three children, Rosemary who had lived in a commune and then married twice, both times to a man with a limp. Come on, Betty, they called, I dare you, come on. Don't go in the dark with a boy, don't let me catch you. No one will have you if you don't keep yourself nice, you know what I mean.

Who wouldn't be a little crazy, she asked Caidin, who was standing quiet beside her, looking into the tunnel. But as everyone knew, if you could ask the question, you were all right. Caidin licked her hand and they both looked into the tunnel. Its bricks were maybe a little darker than they had been the last time, very beautiful really, against the new green of the trees. She remembered the touch of a hand on her hand, her shoulder, her cheek, and she closed her eyes to make it more real, that time when her body was perfect, if only she had known it.

There were probably never many more than 100 residents, and almost all of them were exclusively miners and their families. There was a row of houses along the railroad tracks, a sawmill, schoolhouse, post office, general store, and a saloon. The last family left in 1947, by the 1960s all of the buildings were gone.... ohiotres-passers.com

Taylor was singing a new song, but only in her head. She sang it to Laurette, her mouth against Laurette's ear, but not moving her lips. We're going to Moonville, she sang, we're going to live in Moonville. Moonville is full of the moon. She was riding on her father's shoulders, bobbing up and down, all the landscape around her bobbing as he walked up the trail. She let her head bob even more so that her chin banged her chest.

What's going to be there? she asked. What will we see?

Just a tunnel, baby. There's a tunnel and a crick.

Can I go in the water?

We'll see.

Laurette can't go in the water. It'd wreck her innards.

Her father laughed. Maybe you can't either. It might be too cold.

It would wreck her innards, she thought, she'd be as cold as in the refrigerator. Cold as a mackerel, her grandmother said sometimes. A mackerel was a fish.

Will there be houses?

Not any more, her father said.

No lambs, no houses. They were gone. Taylor wriggled her toes in her shoes, getting ready to take them off for the crick, which was water, and not like a crick in the neck.

Some of the letters were still sharp, the M, the E. But in the middle, the OO was softened, worn down. Irene's mother told stories about going there to picnic, crossing over the creek on the trestle. She said once she was there with her sister when the train still came through, and that they had heard it coming, but somehow ignored it or thought it was something else. The train came and they had to jump, but it was OK, for they were almost at the end of the trestle. If she hadn't been quick enough, there would have been no Irene, she'd said, laughing, although Irene couldn't see that it was funny.

No Irene, she said to Caidin, and then what would you do? You'd belong to Tom now. But then if she hadn't married Tom, would

Tom have bought a dog that, as it turned out, he didn't like? Never mind, she told herself, the past was fixed, at least. You could count on it, no matter how horrible it might have been.

Her mother had said that they used to find bits of old teacups in Raccoon Creek, but that hadn't happened for a long time. Teacups from Moonville, plates, painted with violets and roses. Her mother had thrown them away, she said, another thing that Irene held against her, that she never kept things, that she had no sentiment.

She sat down where she could see both the tunnel and the creek.

The tunnel originally made by stone cutters from huge sandstone blocks. Refurbished with clay bricks in 1903-4. Tunnel about 30-40 ft high, 20-30 feet wide (across the bottom, close to 100 yards long). Some of the original sandstone can be seen at either end. The Moonville Ghost Web Ring

Roger was showing off, leaping up the trail, bounding out to scare Evie, howling like a dog. Who was the kid here, really. He said she was immature when she didn't want to have sex, or complained about not going out to a fancy place for dinner. If we love each other, those things don't matter, he said to her. Evie kept what she felt locked in her own head. She didn't think it was love. Love was joy, she thought, a desperate waiting, a falling together that went on and on. She hoped she'd kept her head straight about all that, no matter what she was doing with Roger.

Look here, Evie. Roger caught her arm and pulled her off the path.

What, she said. She pulled out her cigarettes and lit one.

It's a pawpaw tree. We used to have them on the farm.

We who? she said, meaning to be snotty. But he ignored her. You can shake them down from the trees when they're ripe.

Evie put her cigarette between her lips and took the tree in both hands, shaking as hard as she could. Far above her the thin limbs of the tree shimmied and rustled.

Not now, Roger said, they're not ripe now. There's nothing there until September maybe. They fall from the tree when they're ready.

But not now, Evie said. She drew sharply in on the cigarette before taking it out of her mouth. It was never now. Evie rolled her eyes. Whatever.

Taylor dabbled her fingers in the brown water. Her father was sitting on a rock, smoking, looking away, like he did sometimes. She sat Laurette down on the grass and started taking off her shoes. They pinched a little and she wriggled her toes in her socks, and then took off the socks. Laurette had shoes, too, and she took them off and set the four shoes in a row.

Now you see, Laurette, she said in a small breathy voice, you just put your feet in to see if it's cold. Laurette felt that it was cold, but Taylor was stern. You'll get used to it in a minute, see if you don't.

Laurette's skirt floated on the water like a flower. You'll see, it's going to be nice. Taylor edged toward the water, letting her toes feel the surface. The crick was running along fast and bubbly, leaves floating like little boats. She stretched her legs and inched forward.

Irene's knees hurt, and she felt that one of her headaches might be starting, but the grass was soft under her. She watched the welcoming dark of the tunnel entrance, thinking of old times. A bonfire, the passing of a bottle, the search for a soft spot. Her young body bent under someone's mouth. Her mother's face in those years, boxed and prim. Irene's belief in herself (although she was Betty then), her conviction that nothing could hurt her. Her hair had been long and pale brown, never dyed (for her mother wouldn't allow it), but now she saw that it had been as nice a color as blonde in its way. She had cut it for the wedding, as if it were a requirement for marriage to Tom, a stiffly sprayed bouffant like a helmet. Caidin was running toward her now, barking and she got onto her knees, pushing against the ground to raise herself up. Was he hurt? Someone was chasing him, and Irene's heart twisted in her chest.

There it is. Roger waved his hand like a magician, and in spite of herself, Evie felt eager, light, as if a curtain would draw back and reveal something she'd been dreaming of since she was a little girl. She'd been a dopy kid, she knew now, always wanting to be a ballerina or some shit like that. Ahead she could see something dark rising above and behind the trees, and she began to run.

Wait now, Roger called. She could hear him lumbering behind her but she didn't stop, she ran all out like she used to when she was ten. He sounded angry but he was old and he couldn't catch her, he'd have to stop and get his breath or he'd probably have a heart attack. She broke through the trees and there it was, the stone walls dark against the sky. A white dog was coming out of the dark mouth of the tunnel like a bullet, and a woman was crying out. Evie laughed, for it was so much better than she'd expected, the noise, the light and darkness, the drama. The dog ran toward her and she opened her arms to it.

Sound travels well in the tunnel. When a person whispers from one end of the tunnel, it can be heard all the way at the other side. Visitor Information Brochure, Lake Hope State Park.

Taylor's feet were wet, which was bad. You'll catch your death Aunt Amy said when she stepped in a puddle. Taylor could hear someone yelling. Her father looked up and then stood. Don't worry, she told Laurette. Her father was looking the other way, and she pushed Laurette into the water. You're drowning but don't worry, she said. To save her she had to get all the way in.

"The ghost of Moonville, after an absence of one year, has returned and is again at its old pranks, haunting B&O S-W freight trains and their crews. It appeared Monday night in front of fast freight No. 99 west bound, just east of the cut which is one half mile the other side of Moonville at the point where Engineer Law-head lost his life and Engineer Walters was injured. The ghost, attired in a pure white robe, carried a lantern. It had a flowing white beard, its eyes glistened like balls of fire and surrounding it was a halo of twinkling stars. When the train stopped, the ghost stepped off the track and disappeared into the rocks nearby...." The Chillicothe Gazette, 1895

Irene panted, trying to catch her breath. A young girl was holding Caidin, he was licking her face, and she was laughing. She had long brown hair that twined and tangled in Caidin's beautiful silvery-white fur, and for a minute, Irene felt that she might be looking at herself, the ghost of her young self, the self who had not cut her hair, had not married Tom. The one who hadn't listened so closely to her mother, who would not let herself be eaten up by cancer and grief. Her hand went to her chest, feeling for the empty place. She felt invisible, caught in a piece of unfriendly time, unable to move toward Caidin or reclaim him.

But it was just a girl, of course, a girl who was studded with silver hoops, even her nose and her navel. Caidin, Irene called, and was sad to hear her voice so weak and quavery.

She heard a voice call back. Betty, it called, and she thought how strange it was to hear Caidin's voice after all this time, a gravely baritone, as if he'd been a smoker. He knew her old name, of course, there was no hiding anything from him.

The water was cold, like when her father filled the baby pool from the hose. Taylor had a hold of Laurette, and she splashed in the water. Swimming was like jumping or like lying down on the water while your legs kicked. See, she said to Laurette, but the water splashed up into her mouth. The water was foamy, like her bath water with bubbles in it, and it seemed like it was in a hurry to go someplace. Don't worry, Taylor said to Laurette, but she felt a little worried herself. She remembered baby Brooke who was supposed to be looking out for her. But maybe she had other stuff to do in heaven. Maybe she was sleeping. And anyway, what could she do? She was just a stupid baby.

Evie laughed. The dog was licking her, as if they had always known each other. She heard Roger call out, and ignored him. Aren't you beautiful, she said to the dog. Aren't you the prettiest puppy in the world.

Roger was calling out someone's name, not hers. Betty Ferris, he was calling. Is that you? Evie hoped Betty wasn't one of his wife's friends or she'd never hear the end of it. But who cares, she said to the dog, pulling his ears gently. The dog opened his mouth and took her hand gently between his teeth, pulling.

Roger and some old lady were talking, and she let herself be led away. Let him look for her, serve him right for paying attention to old Betty. She could have him, Evie thought, and as if she had been thinking of this all along, she knew she was going to break up with him.

With a great sense of relief, she followed the dog down the bank to the creek. On the grassy verge, a man was pulling off his shoes, calling out something. He struggled with the shoes, and when Evie came up to him, he turned to her and said, can you swim? My god, can you swim? I can't swim. He seemed prepared to jump in if she said no, so she told the truth. I was on the swim team, she said, and he pointed downstream.

Something pink and white floating in the river, like a bouquet thrown away by a bride. It's Taylor, he said, my god, she's in the water.

Evie jumped in, and the dog followed her.

The far western portion of Hocking County drains into Raccoon Creek, which is in some places as deep as 30 feet, flowing eventually to the Ohio River. It's a geological phenomenon, one of several stream reversals caused by the glaciers. old-eforester.com

Betty Ferris? Not Caidin (of course!), but a man, heavy in the shoulders, brushcut hair. Is that you? he said. It used to be me, Irene said, and then added Yes, for clarity. It was someone she knew, or used to know.

Roger Hardesty, he was saying, and she found herself blushing, for she had known him in high school (how could she have forgotten?), Logan High School, all those many years ago. How nice, she said, remembering that he'd sat in front of her in her junior year history class, remembering even the plaid of his shirts drawn close over the muscle of his back, how his shoulders shifted when he slumped in his chair. It's Irene now, she said, but he didn't seem to hear her.

Betty Ferris, he said. What are you doing out here?

Walking my dog, she said. What about you?

Hiking, he said, but he seemed embarrassed.

Under his gaze, she felt first younger and then older, conscious of her thinned hair, her scrawniness. My dog, Caidin, she said, and looked around for him. He was gone, and so was the girl who'd been hugging him.

Evie cut through the water. She could see the child, a bundle of sodden clothes, ahead, bobbing up and going under. She came to the rapids and scrambled over the rocks, slipping on their algaed sides, the water foaming around her ankles. The dog dove into the deeper pool ahead, and she went in his wake, swimming as if she were lane-to-lane with her fiercest rival, Tiffany Lewis. She'd given it up when she hooked up with Roger—he often had free time when there was a practice. What was I, crazy? she thought. The water was like silk, or like Jello, and she moved through it with her powerful crawl (second place in State's).

She followed the curve of the creek and when she came around the little bluff of trees the water smoothed out. She could feel the deep of it under her. The little girl and her pink and white clothes had disappeared. Evie looked to the white dog as if for advice. His eyes were blue, and they seemed to signal her. He bobbed his head and dove under the silty brown water.

Heaven was green, Taylor saw, green and ghostly, long trails of things coming up from the dark below. Brooke was waiting for her, and Taylor tried to shake her head. She didn't like the green, or the taste of the water in her mouth. She didn't like baby Brooke. Heaven was wet. Laurette's dress would be ruined. Dolls did not go to heaven, Aunt Amy said, and that was that. Dolls were not in the Bible, she said. But Laurette was here, so what did Aunt Amy know?

Taylor was tired, and her hair was drifting around her as she sank. The tangles would never come out.

In the Moonville Cemetery, I noticed that a lot of the graves we found were of the last name Jones.... A lot of the gravestones had "Asleep with Jesus" imprinted on them. The graves were surprisingly in very good condition for being well over 100 years old. home.fuse.net/Moonville

Irene brushed her hands down the front of her pants. How have you been? She wished she'd combed her hair. I didn't recognize you at first, she said.

You've still got those green eyes, Roger said. Are you still married to what's his name? Tom?

Oh, no, Irene said. That's all over. She waved her hand. One of those things.

A man was running up from the river. He didn't have any shoes on, Irene noticed, which was strange. Have you got a signal? he said. Can you call 911?

I have a satellite phone, Roger said. What's wrong?

She's gone in the river, the man said. I just turned around for a minute and she was gone.

Who? Irene said, but they were already running down to the creek. Where? she said. The man gestured downstream, but there was nothing to be seen. Roger was talking into his phone, and the man started to run down the bank, pushing through the brush.

Irene's heart was beating fast. Where was Caidin? He wasn't in sight. Caidin, she called, but he didn't bark in answer. She'd lost so many things, she couldn't bear to lose anymore, not one more thing. Caidin, she called again, screaming as loud as she could. Roger, still talking on the phone, reached out and took her hand.

Evie followed the dog, but once under the surface she couldn't see much, just the silt hanging in the water like clouds in the sky, obscuring the light. The trees overhung the river, darkening the water. It felt as if night was coming, the dark night where the moon didn't reach. The moon in Moonville, which was silly, she thought. She came up for air, and the water spread around her as smooth as a plate, only the ripples of her surfacing to disturb it. She felt at home in the river, the water like thicker air, holding her up. She could hear voices from upstream, someone calling a word that sounded like "fading," as if they were commenting on the passing of the light. It would be night in a little while. She didn't find this displeasing, but she had to find the dog, and they had to do what they were there for.

There were at least four deaths near the tunnel, including a young girl who was killed by a passing train on the nearby trestle while going to visit a lover. ohiotrespassers.com

God was supposed to be in Heaven, Taylor thought, but he wasn't. No God, no Brooke. But there were angels, with teeth. One of them took her by the neck of her blouse and dragged her through the green cloudy light. She tried to say that it hurt but her mouth was full of water. She fell out of Heaven still holding Laurette and the angel pulled her along the surface of the sky. Someone put an arm around her and she and the angel pulled until she felt Heaven falling away, going down like the water in the tub. Her father stood ahead, holding out his arms, and Taylor was happy that he wanted to keep her with him.

When Irene and Roger got there, the brown-haired girl was bent over a child lying on the bank, water dribbling out of her mouth. The shoeless man knelt with his hands clasped as if he were in church. Caidin lay watching the girl press the water from the still, silent body and breathe into her mouth.

The paramedics are on their way, Roger said. They stood, hands hanging loose, unable to move, listening to the girl's ragged breathing, and the steady puffs of air she pushed into the little girl's mouth.

Oh, Irene thought, if anyone, it should be me. She ought to offer herself, she thought, to say, take me instead of this child. Roger was still holding her hand, and she wanted to step away from him, but his hand was so warm, so almost familiar that she hesitated. It should be me, she thought, feeling the lightness and space next to her heart. But she couldn't pray for it, she couldn't give herself to the thought. She didn't want to give Death even this advantage, the edge of her selfless wish.

Taylor opened her eyes, although she hadn't realized they were closed. The sky was in the right place, the creek was beside her, talking to itself. Her father was crying, which men weren't supposed to do.

Do I know you? she asked the girl who had been kissing her. Her father was falling down on her, and she put her arms around him.

I'm Evie, she said to the little girl. Evie sat back on her heels, panting almost as hard as the dog. Her hair was probably a mess. She pushed it back from her face and looked around for Roger.

Are you OK? he said.

A lot you care, she said, but she couldn't help smiling. He was an asshole and it was over, but he wasn't so bad.

What's your name? she said to the little girl. She gave her the doll to hold, and its hard-lashed eyes clicked open. I'm Taylor, she said, and this is Laurette. She's been very bad, but it'll be OK after she goes in timeout.

Evie laughed. The white dog looked up at her, panting, his teeth gleaming. Water dripped from her hair. The creek kept sliding past them, coming down from Moonville.

ABOUT THE AUTHOR

Mary Grimm has had two books published – a novel, *Left to Themselves* and a story collection, *Stealing Time*. Her stories have appeared in *The New Yorker*, *Antioch Review*, and *Mississippi Review*, among others, and her flash fiction in places like *Helen, Berlin Fiction Kitchen*, and *Tiferet*. Currently, she is working on a series of climate change novellas.

MARY GRIMM

C&R PRESS TITLES

NONFICTION & MEMOIR

Afterlife of a Kept Boy by Dale Corvino
From the Womb of Sky and Earth by Leslie Contreras Schwartz
This is Infertility by Kirsten McLennan
Curriculum Vitae by Gregory de la Haba
Many Paths by Bruce McEver
By the Bridge or By the River by Amy Roma
Gatbsy's Child by Dorin Schumacher
Women in the Literary Landscape by Doris Weatherford, et al

FICTION

Transcendent Gardening by Ed Falco
Juniper Street by Joan Frank
All I Should Not Tell by Brian Leung
A History of the Cat by Anis Shivani
Pages from the Textbook of an Alternate History
        by Phong Nguyen
No Good, Very Bad Asian by Lelund Cheuk
Last Tower to Heaven by Jacob Paul
Surrendering Appomattox by Jacob M. Appel
Headlong by Ron MacLean
A Diet of Worms by Erik Rasmussen
The Pleasures of Queuing by Erik Martiny
Life During Wartime by Katie Rogin
Cloud Diary by Steve Mitchell
Ivy vs. Dogg by Brian Leung
While You Were Gone by Sybil Baker
Made by Mary by Laura Catherine Brown
Spectrum by Martin Ott
That Man in Our Lives by Xu Xi

SHORT FICTION

A Goat Even it Flies by Tariq al Haydar
Transubtatntion by Mary Grimm
A Mother's Tale & Other Stories by Khanh Ha
Fathers of Cambodian Time-Travel Science by Bradley Bazzle
Two Californias by Robert Glick
Meditations on the Mother Tongue by An Tran
The Protester Has Been Released by Janet Sarbanes

ESSAY AND CREATIVE NONFICTION

In the Room of Persistent Sorry by Kristina Marie Darling
the internet is for real by Chris Campanioni
Credo by Rita Banerjee and Diana Norma Szokolyai
Je suis l'autre by Kristina Marie Darling
Immigration Essays by Sybil Baker
Death of Art by Chris Campanioni

POETRY

Curare by Lucian Mattison
Leaving the Skin on the Bear by Kelli Allen
How to Kill Youself Instead of Your Children
        byQuincy Scott Jones
Lottery of Inimacies by Jonathan Katz
What Feels Like Love by Tom C. Hunley
The Rented Altar by Lauren Berry
Communicatingroups by Stu Watson
Between the EArth and Sky by Eleanor Kedney
What Need Have We for Such as We by Amanda Auerbach
Give a Girl Chaos by Heidi Seaborn
The Miracles by Amy Lemmon
Banjo's Inside Coyote by Kelli Allen
A Family is a House by Dustin Pearson

Millenial Roost by Dustin Pearson
Objects in Motion by Jonathan Katz
My Stunt Double by Travis Denton
Dark Horse by Kristina Marie Darling
Lessons in Camoflauge by Martin Ott
Notes to the Beloved by Michelle Bitting
Negro Side of the Moon by Earl Braggs
Ex Domestica by E.G. Cunningham
All My Heroes are Broke by Ariel Francisco
Like Lesser Gods by Bruce McEver
Les Fauves by Barbara Crooker
Imagine Not Drowning by Kelli Allen
Tall as You are Tall Between Them by Annie Christain
Free Boat: Collected Lies and Love Poems by John Reed
The Couple Who Fell to Earth by Michelle Bitting

ART

East Village Closed by Billy the Artist
Things You Don't Here Twice by Billy the Artist
Casanova Erotica by Sonia Hensler